Breaking YOU

A BLACKTHORN ELITE NOVEL

USA Today Bestselling Author

J. L. BECK
C. HALLMAN

1

WARREN

*T*hree years... three fucking years, I have been trying to get her out of my head. Fucking my way through the female population, trying to forget she ever existed. Three years, since I laid eyes on her beautiful face and perfect little body. Three years since I smelt the flowery scent of her hair or tasted the sweetness that always seemed to linger on her lips.

Three years, and there she stands... right in front of me, in the middle of the cafeteria, on *my* fucking campus. I didn't think it was possible, but she looks even more beautiful than the last time I saw her. Even from a distance, I can see she's grown into her body, shapely chest, curves, and legs I could've pictured wrapped around my waist.

Fuck that. The thought leaves my mind throbbing. That was before. Now I wouldn't touch her if she was the last fucking girl on the planet.

She turns to me then, and our eyes lock. Like two magnets drawn to each other in a sea of polar opposites. I hate that I'm drawn to her. Her hazel eyes widen, and I know the exact second recognition sets in. The next second, she looks away, breaking the connection.

In an instant, I become someone else. Just like that, my switch flips. I turn into a darker version of myself, a version that feeds on the pain she caused me. I loved her, trusted her, and she betrayed all of that. She betrayed me.

I'll never forget the way she looked at me that day, the image is ingrained into my mind. She looked so sad and confused as her family drove off my parents' estate. I wanted to hurt her, crush her like a fly, but I refrained. Being content with sending her away and never seeing her again. My silence over her betrayal was enough for me.

She knew what she had done, there was no coming back from that kind of lie. I tried to reason with myself, tried to say there was no way it was true, but the proof was there. In black and white.

"Who is she?" Parker asks, pulling me out of the haze I was in.

"She's no one," I snap, showing more of my true colors than I intended.

"Dude, she's obviously someone. I've never seen your face change so quickly. It was almost like you were seeing a ghost."

I force a smile, but I wouldn't be surprised if it looks more like a snarl. "That's because I was. She's no one, nothing. Forget you saw her." I don't want Parker to get involved in this. Not wanting to talk about it with my best friend any longer, I jump up from my seat and head toward Harper.

Everything around me fades away, the clanking of lunch dishes, the gossiping girls I pass on my way over to her. All I can see is her. I zero in on Harper, like she is the only person in this large room.

Just as I get within earshot, she turns again, almost as if

she's sensed me coming. Her entire body goes rigid, and she takes a tiny step backward.

I almost smile. *Be afraid. Be very afraid.* My muscles burn with energy, and my fingers itch to touch her. Will I hurt her?

"What the hell are you doing here?" I growl.

"I-I go to s-school here," she stutters, holding onto her backpack strap like her life depends on it.

"No, you're not," I order. Circling her arm with my fingers, I pull her out of the cafeteria and through the doors that lead out to the garden, keeping my hold tight.

"Let me go," she whisper-yells, her eyes darting around the room like someone might see and help her. Doesn't she know, no one will save her? That no one in this school can touch me or any of the other guys in our little group? Probably not, but she will, soon enough. Ignoring her struggles, I push forward, tugging her through the black double doors and outside. Eyes burn over my skin as we walk out, but it doesn't bother me. I don't give a flying fuck if the whole school knows what's going on.

By the time I'm done with her, her reputation, and whatever rumor is spread after this will be the least of her worries.

"Warren, stop, you're hurting me." So sweet, so soft, and sing-song like. That voice, it used to be able to get me to do anything, but now, I just want to wrap my hands around her throat and get her to stop talking. Get the memories of us out of my mind.

Tugging her through the grass, I stop once we reach one of the sitting areas next to the vine-covered brick wall. She trips over her feet, nearly falling to the ground before catching herself. She looks up at me, her eyes wide, her chest rising and falling rapidly, I can see her pulse throbbing in her throat.

"You think this hurts?" I squeeze her arm a little tighter

before shoving it away. Then like a lion, I stalk toward her. She, of course, takes a step back until she's reached the wall, leaving herself nowhere to go. I hold back a bitter laugh. She's making this too easy.

"W-what are you doing?" Her lips quiver as I place my hands flat against the wall behind her. Caging her in, I invade her personal space, giving her no room to breathe. No place to hide. Nowhere to run. She shivers, and I love the sight of her scared and weak. Her sweet floral scent assaults my nostrils, and I force myself to breathe through my mouth.

"You made a big mistake coming here. This is my turf. You need to leave and don't fucking come back. One warning, Harper, that's all you're getting." I shouldn't even give her that, but I'm feeling generous, feeling like giving her an out.

She shakes her head, and silky brown strands of hair fall into her face, "I have a scholarship to go to *this* school. I can't just leave. And what does it matter? How was I supposed to know that you would be here?"

My jaw ticks, she has a fucking backbone. Yet, another thing I'll take pleasure in breaking if she stupidly decides to stay.

"I don't give a shit about how you got here; all I care about is making you disappear. You need to leave. *Now*."

Shoving against my chest, she tries to push past me. "Get out of the way." Even through the shirt I'm wearing, her touch burns my skin. Her push just moves me closer to the edge. Determined to get my point across, I grab both her wrists and shove them against her chest, holding them there.

"Leave, and I'll forget that you ever showed your face here. Stay, and I'll break you so badly you'll leave a shell of the person you are now. Either way, you're going to leave."

She visibly gulps, her throat bobbing, and I want to trace

that delicate throat of hers, feel the flutter of her heartbeat under my fingers.

Digging deep, she stands a little straighter and fights against my hold. "You're insane, I'm not leaving, and you can't make me. We don't even know each other anymore, and me being here has no effect on you. Now let go of me before I report you to the campus police."

I laugh right in her face, "Do it. That would be hilarious."

"What happened to you?" she whispers the words so soft I'm sure she didn't intend to speak them out loud.

Leaning into her face, I keep an inch of space between our faces. "I don't think I'm required to tell you a single fucking thing. But because you asked so nicely, I'll tell you. What happened to me was *you*. I want you gone." I bare my teeth. I want to bite her and mark her skin.

"I'm not leaving, Warren." The way she says my name, all breathless and shit, it does something to me. It's like she is poking the monster inside of me. Awakening it with nothing but her voice.

I don't even think, all I do is react. Releasing her hands, I slam my fist into the brick beside her head, nearly hitting her in the process, and I use my other hand to grip her chin between two fingers. I pinch hard, and the blood swooshes in my ears when I see her wince. I should feel something, anything, but I don't. The idea of hurting her...it only makes my cock harder, makes the blood in my veins heat.

"You know what this means then, don't you?" I seethe, barely restraining myself. Her full bee-stung lips are right in front of me, begging to be kissed.

Wide-eyed, she shakes her head once more, and her chin wobbles in my grasp, giving away her fear. Good, I want her to be afraid. I want her a trembling mess beneath my feet.

Looking at her once more, I memorize her body, dragging my predatory gaze over her. I want to strip her bare and fuck her until she screams.

No. I roar internally. I can't let her get under my skin. I can't give in to my weaknesses.

"I'm going to break you, crush you until you're begging me to take mercy on your pitiful body." Releasing her chin, I turn and stalk off, knowing that if I don't, I might do something I'll regret. I want to scare her, hurt her, but not physically. I fist my hands so tightly that my fingernails dig into my palm, probably piercing through the skin. I don't care though. The pain is just what I need to continue onward.

With each step I take away from her, my blood cools a little more, and my mind clears. Slowly, I return to the Warren everyone knows me as; the all American boy with a panty-melting smile and enough charm to leave the ladies dazed and confused.

Revenge. I'll get my revenge, but first, I need to get some information on her. Find out what will make her disappear as fast as she came here.

2

HARPER

With the back of my hand, I wipe some sweat off my forehead as I finish unpacking the very last box. *Finally.* It took me long enough. Then again, considering I moved my entire life without having any help, I guess I didn't do so bad after all.

My one-room apartment is small and shabby, but it's mine. By one room, I don't mean one bedroom, plus a kitchen, and a living room. No, I mean one room all together, and no, it's not a huge space either. It's only ten by fifteen square feet. It's a little better than a jail cell. My bed is in one corner, while a desk and chair are in the other. Next to the entrance door is a tiny kitchenette with a two-plate stove, a mini-fridge, and a microwave.

The only other room that is part of the apartment is the attached bathroom, which is just big enough to hold a sink, a shower stall, and a toilet. Did I mention the tiles in that said bathroom are green and pink? Yeah, I know, disgusting.

I've put everything into unpacking over the last couple of hours so that I didn't have to think about the events of earlier today. Shivers wrack my body as I recall the darkness in his eyes, the hate that pulsed just below like lava bubbling up to the surface. I could feel it, it coated the air, making it hard for me to breathe.

"*I'm going to break you, crush you until you're begging me to take mercy on your pitiful body.*" His words wash over me, playing on repeat in my mind like a never-ending song. Moving away from the box, I sag down onto my bed, the mattress squeaking as I do.

Warren is here. I don't think that reality has sunk in yet. And he hates me, really hates me, and I don't understand why. What have I done to him? The last time I saw him, we were sixteen, and I was in the back of my parents' car driving away from his family's mansion. For years, I wondered why he never said goodbye, how he could go from caring about me so much, to despising me in the blink of an eye.

I thought maybe it was the fact that I was the maid's daughter, but that never seemed to bother him. Maybe he changed his mind? My parents always warned me, told me that we would never work out, his family had money, and mine had nothing. I didn't listen. I loved Warren, and I thought he loved me. *Pfft, what a lie that was.*

Seeing him today awakened feelings in me I've tried to forget for years. In fact, I've tried to forget him altogether, but I never could. I tried to date but never made it past a first kiss. That's usually when I realized that the guy wouldn't ever measure up to Warren.

I kept waiting for that spark, that excitement I used to get when kissing Warren, but it never came with anyone else, and I'm not sure if it ever will. Which means I'll never feel that spark again since Warren clearly has no interest in ever being with me again. I don't know why, but that bothers me. I shouldn't still want him, but I do. Like a moth drawn to a flickering flame, I don't care about burning, if it gets me a little closer to him.

Absentmindedly, my hand comes up to my face, and my fingers brush over my chin, where he touched me earlier. The skin there still tingles, like he has left a part of himself behind. Branded my skin with his touch. The thought sends a rush of euphoric need through me. I still want him, even though I shouldn't.

Shaking the thought of him away, I roll over and reach under my bed, feeling around for my special box. When my fingers touch the smooth edge of the shoe box, I grab it and pull it out.

Still halfway hanging off the bed, I open the lid and look at my small but diverse collection of dildos and vibrators. The miniature purple one has always been my favorite. It's small but packs quite the vibrating punch. And that's what I need right now. Something that will kick Warren right out of my mind and make my toes curl in the process.

With a smile on my lips, I place the vibrator next to me on the bed. Lying flat on my back, I shimmy out of my yoga pants and panties, kicking them both to the floor when they reach my ankles. Falling back onto my pillow, I reach for *Roger*, that's what I call my little purple friend. I can already feel the tension easing out of me.

Closing my eyes, I turn on Roger and let my legs fall apart. Bringing the vibrator to my clit, I draw circles with the tip, teasing myself. My blood hums and pleasure blooms deep in my belly. I keep the vibration on low for now, almost like my little private foreplay.

When I can't stand waiting any longer, I push the vibrator lower and into my opening. I'm already wet, so it slides in with ease, and a shudder ripples through me at the movement. Even though I'm alone, I bite my lip to stifle the moan trying to escape my lips.

Moving the vibrator in and out, I up the speed and let the pulses of vibration buzz through me. It doesn't take long before the sound of my arousal fills my ears. I'm so wet, I should be embarrassed. Closing my eyes, an image of Warren pops into my mind. I can feel his hands on me, his knuckles skimming against my wet folds.

"*Look at this mess. You're all fucking wet... what will I do with you now?*" My pulse quickens, and my pussy quivers, my body on the edge of an orgasm.

"Oh, god..." I pant into the empty room, fucking myself faster and faster.

"*Come, show me how much your pussy craves my cock...show me, Harper...*" I squeeze my eyes closed tighter, and air rapidly enters my lungs as I fall over the edge and into stormy waters to the sound of Warren's deep angry voice. I let the waves of pleasure wrap around me, tugging me deeper and deeper. My heart races, and I do my best to focus on the pleasure and not the fact that I just came to imagining his voice.

I've barely come down from my high when a loud knock fills the room. For a moment, I'm paralyzed, still suspended in time. *Is someone at the door?* I can't be sure, my mind hasn't fully returned to this room yet. Part of it is still somewhere up in the clouds.

"Open the door, Harper. I know you're in there. You can't hide forever," my cousin Valerie's voice pierces through the lustful fog around my head. I'm up, scrabbling to find my pants and pull them on before she kicks the door in. Seriously, she would do it. I've finally got everything into place when I start walking toward the door. Then I remember the vibrator is still on and sitting on the bed. *Shit.*

"Do you want to pay for a new door because I will seriously kick..."

Rushing over to the bed, I turn the thing off and stuff it under my pillow before jogging back over to the front door. I tuck any loose strands of hair behind my ear and unlock the door, opening it slowly. I know before Valerie even says anything that I look guilty. My cheeks are blazing, and my insides are knotted. What's the point of masturbating if I didn't get to enjoy the aftershocks?

Valerie eyes me like she's a detective. "What were you doing?" She questions walking into the small space with her arms crossed over her chest, and her eyes narrowed.

Rolling my eyes, I close the door, "Nothing, Val, unpacking and getting used to the place."

"Hmmm." She nibbles on her bottom lip. "Why are you so sweaty?"

Self-consciously, I look down at the floor. "I'm not, and if I am, it's because of all the moving."

"Right, like I believe that." She busts out with laughter. Looking up from the floor, I see she's straightened her silky brown hair and painted her face on.

"What do you want? I thought you had plans, and that's why you couldn't do Chinese with me?" I try not to sound upset about it, but I kind of am. After the crap with Warren, I really could've used someone to talk to right away. Valerie, of course, said she had plans, and I wasn't going to spill my guts about Warren to her over the phone.

"No longer is it me that has plans but *us.*" Her thick brown eyebrows wiggle back and forth, and I know whatever it is that's including *us,* I'm not going to like.

"What are these plans you have because if it involves boys, booze, or birth control, I'm not game." I purse my lips and stare at her head-on. Valerie and I couldn't be any different. Yes, we look similar, both of us having the same silky brown hair and light hazel eyes, but outside of that, there is no comparison. I'm a straight A student, grades and blazing a path for myself have always been the most important things to me.

Drinking, partying, and sleeping around have been Valerie's. Since she was a teenager, she's been trouble, and college life was merely a gateway to all of her favorite events. Valerie doesn't go to school here, neither does she want to. She chose the local community college, and honestly, I was surprised by that. To finance her school, she works as a waitress at a local burger joint, which she claims she loves because of the great tips. I can hardly believe that since waitresses barely make anything.

"There is a party at one of the frat boys' houses. I always go alone but want you to go with me tonight. It'll be good for you, let you check out all the guys, and maybe make some friends? I don't go to school here, so I can't help you during the day, and we both know you could use the extra help with making friends."

Gritting my teeth, I prepare to deny her claim, but really, she isn't wrong. Since moving away, I've found it hard—if not impossible—to maintain friendships. Maybe because of the way things ended with Warren, or maybe it was because I had to start over as a sophomore at a different high school. I don't know. I just never got a chance to really click with anyone. That doesn't mean that the *friends* I want are going to be at this party though.

"I need to make friends with people that care about their

grades and studying, not people who are focused on chugging a beer the fastest or who slept with who last."

Valerie frowns, "Will you just come and stop being such a downer. You're nineteen, but you act like you're ninety. Live a little."

Live a little? I scoff. Valerie has lived enough for at least five college freshman girls. I'm okay living inside my bubble away from the rest of the world. Nonetheless, if I don't go, she will continue to beg and plead, and truthfully, I could use a drink even if it is stale frat boy beer.

"Fine, I'll go," as soon as the words pass my lips, I regret them.

"Oh, my god. Yes!" Valerie squeals, jumping up and down in her heels that look like something a stripper might wear. "I'll do your hair and makeup and make you all sexy. No one with a penis will be able to stop themselves from looking your way."

"No, no, and also... no."

"Yes, yes, yes! I'm not taking no for an answer."

"If I go with you to this party and let you use me as a human doll, will you leave me alone for the rest of the year?"

"The year?" Valerie throws her hands in the air dramatically. "How about I'll leave you alone for the rest of the semester?"

"Deal," I sigh in defeat. I don't know why I'm even agreeing to this, probably because I've always had a hard time saying no to Val. Today is no different. I just hope I don't run into Warren at this party. Then again, these are Valerie's friends. What are the chances of *him* being there anyway?

3

WARREN

Two chicks take their shirts off and streak through the crowded living room. Tits and booze. That's what the night can be summed up with. Bringing the cup to my lips, I tip back the remaining beer inside of it and swallow it down. It helps drown out my thoughts of her... *Harper*. My forever, my forbidden, my fucking weakness.

Music blasts through the space, the smell of smoke, cheap beer, and expensive perfume permeate the air. I squeeze the red solo cup in my hand, the plastic cracking against the pressure. The place is brimming with people, and yet, I couldn't feel anymore alone. Parker, of course, didn't come with me tonight, being pussy-whipped and all.

My eyes dance over the makeshift dance floor in the center of the room, each chick gyrating her hips a possible candidate for riding my dick. I could have any of them, but none of them are drawing me in.

Cameron and Easton, two of my best friends outside of Parker, flank me, one on each side, one with a chick of their choice plastered to their side.

"The pussy's good for the taking tonight..." Cameron snickers in my ear, a shit-eating grin on his face. All I can do is shrug. Since discovering Harper is at Blackthorn, I've had a hard time looking at other chicks, almost like I'm not interested in anyone else but her. Which is fucking stupid. Harper means nothing to me. She's worthless, dirt beneath my feet, she lost her worth the day I found out she betrayed me. When I found out the kind of girl, she really was.

I should've known. I should've fucking known. My father had been warning me about girls like her my whole fucking life, reminding me of what happens when you fall for the wrong woman.

"Dude, the cup's already crushed. You okay?" Easton asks, his hand in the pants of the chick that's basically humping his leg.

"Fine, just need another beer." Or five, or a million. I walk away and into the kitchen, needing something stronger. Surveying the bottles of liquor, I contemplate what to drink next. I should just take the bottle of vodka and go outside. Drown myself in the bottom of it. Briefly, I actually consider it, before pushing the thought away. Getting blackout drunk isn't what I need right now.

Instead, I make myself a Captain and Coke and head back out into the living room, ignoring all the other people in the room. I wish I could shut them all up, block out all the noise. It makes me sick to my stomach. Coming here was a bad idea. I should have just stayed home. Ever since Parker decided to make things serious with Willow, it's been hard for me to feel like myself. It feels as though I've lost my partner in crime, and I guess in a way, I did.

I make it a total of maybe five feet before something creeps up my spine. Call it a sixth sense, or a gut reaction, but I could feel her, feel something off in the air. I know she is here. I turn my head, and my eyes find her immediately. There she stands in the center of the room, surrounded by dozens of people, but she couldn't stand out anymore if she tried.

For one second, I let myself enjoy the show. Enjoy the way she looks. Delicate, so fucking fragile, she's like a twig, easily breakable.

She's dancing in the middle of the room, her body moving to the music like a professional dancer. Her lips are tipped up at the sides, and even though her eyes are closed, I can tell she is happy, her head is tipped back as she becomes one with the music.

Her hips sway, and my eyes are drawn to that region. Squeezing the plastic in my hands a little harder than I should, I can't help but stare at her perfectly rounded ass. Two perfect globes of flesh. I'm mesmerized by her, caught in her web. The girls I'm used to starve themselves into a size zero until they're left with no ass and no tits.

Harper is the opposite in every way and the perfect shape. Warm and soft, with gentle curves instead of bony hips. A tiny waist, but with nice heavy breasts, and an ass that is just begging to be grabbed and held on to while I fuck her from behind.

Fuck her? No, you fucking idiot. Keep your cock out of her. Digging deep, I find the anger that I've let fester for years. I shove the image before me away and chug down my drink in nothing more than a gulp. I love the heat that coats my insides as the liquor slides down my throat before settling heavy in my stomach. It makes me feel warm all over but doesn't reach my frigid heart. Nah, that's impenetrable, coated in a thick layer of ice since the day she left.

Time to ruin someone's night. Letting the mask of hate slip onto my face, I stomp across the wooden floor, each step heavy, and full of determination.

As I step closer, I realize that there is someone else with her. Valerie, her out of control cousin. A wicked sneer appears on my lips without even trying. Val sees me first, her eyes turning to the size of dinner plates. Her happy demeanor slips off her face instantaneously. *That's right, cower at my feet.* She's never liked me, not when we were kids, and obviously, that hasn't changed, and I can guarantee that her feelings toward me are not going to get better any time soon. Especially not after tonight.

Valerie nudges Harper's arm, forcing her to look in my direction, but by the time Harper does, I'm already in front of her.

"I didn't give you permission to come to this party," I leer because it's the most dickish thing that pops into my mind at that second. She cranes her head back and stares up at me for half a second, before puffing up her chest and placing one hand on her hip. If I didn't hate her so much, I would say the move was kind of cute.

"Good thing I don't need your permission," Harper sasses, her words slurring slightly. Whatever she had to drink must have given her some liquid courage.

"Talk to me like that again, and I'll make sure your mouth is put to better use for the rest of the night," I threaten, already imagining all the things I could do to her and her mouth.

"I don't know what the hell your problem with me is, but I am done with it already. Go away!" Harper presses a finger to my chest, and a bolt of energy zings through me and straight to my cock. I guess it's no longer a threat.

Reaching for her, I wrap my fingers around her slender wrist. She tries to pull away, but my hand resembles an iron shackle. One she won't be breaking so easily. Her angry expression morphs into fear, and I can see her swallow thickly, her lips pressed together in a tight line.

"Let's go," I order, but don't wait for her to move. Instead, I turn and start pulling her toward one of the bathrooms. She doesn't even try to pull away again, just follows me like a lost puppy. I can't help but wonder if she wants this. Did she provoke me on purpose?

Inside the room, I close the door behind us, turning the lock for good measure. The music is now muffled, but not drowned out by any means. I let go of her wrist, and she scurries back a little. I smirk. There is nowhere to run to now.

"I warned you, Harper. Warned you more than once."

She looks up at me, her bottom lip slightly trembling, but her eyes filled with defiance and something else... excitement?

"You can't do this."

"Can't do what?" I take a step toward her, and she takes a step back. I shake my head at her. "You can't run from me. There is nowhere to go."

She takes another step back, her thighs bump against the edge of the tub. Ensnared in my trap. She'll be my next victim, willing or not.

"I'm not having sex with you in here."

I cock my head to the side and examine her features, "Why? You want me to take you to a nice hotel? I think the bathroom is more fitting for your standards." Anger returns to her face, and without warning, she slams both of her hands into my chest.

"You're a fucking asshole. Let me out of here. I'm done playing your games."

"You think this is a game?" I shove her arms away and grip her by the throat. I don't squeeze enough to make it hard for her to breathe, but the threat is there. "I told you, I'll put your mouth to better use, and I don't make idle threats. You'll do what I say because I tell you to. Because if you don't, the consequences are going to be grave."

There's a defiance in her, it's like a flower growing through concrete, more determined than ever to live in an environment that it doesn't belong in.

"I won't break for you," she croaks, and all I can do is smile.

"Break? No, baby, you won't just break, you will fucking shatter." Releasing her throat, I grab onto one of her shoulders and guide her to the floor, none to gently.

As soon as she reaches the floor, I pop the button on my jeans and slide them down enough free my cock.

At the sight of my fully erect length, her eyes bulge. I wonder if the guy who took her the first time was as big as me? Probably not.

"What happened to you?" Her voice is nothing more than a whisper, but her question sparks a raging forest fire of anger inside of me.

"*What happened to me?*" I mock. My fingers dig into her shoulders as I hold her in place. She winces, but I ignore her pain. Maybe that's what she needs to feel the same pain I felt. To feel as used as I did that day when I found out the truth about her.

"Open your mouth," I order, "and if you bite me... it will be the last thing you do with your mouth." A low whimper is the only sound that she makes as I bring the mushroom head of my cock to her lips. My heart stills in my chest, ceasing to exist for one second as I watch it slip into her warm mouth and past her beautiful full lips.

Fuck me. The image is wet dream-worthy, and one I'll store in my spank bank for a while.

Weaving my fingers through her dark mane, I cradle the back of her head. I can't help but wonder how many guys she's fucked or given blow jobs to. A pounding forms inside my head and a memory surfaces. I latch onto it, letting the bitter anger from it wash over me.

"I'm not ready, Warren," Harper sighs against my chest, her legs straddling me. It's been this way for a few weeks now. Every time we get close enough to have sex, she pulls away. It's frustrating as hell and gives me a major case of blue balls, but I want her for more than just sex.

"It's okay, Harp. I love you, regardless. When it's time, it'll happen, until then I'm content with just having you in my arms," I assure her with a gentle kiss.

Like a slingshot being pulled back, I snap out of the memory and thrust hard into her warm mouth. Using both hands, she presses against my muscled thighs. I hold her head in place, my endorphins rising as she struggles against my grasp.

One second. Two seconds. Three seconds. I release her, and she pulls away, tears streaming down her face, and drool dribbling down over her chin. Such a fucking beautiful disaster. I want to paint against her flesh with my come, mark her, breed her. When my eyes connect with hers, fear reflects back at me.

Finally. It's about time she realized that I mean fucking business. When I reach for her to bring her mouth back to my cock, she flinches. That single movement reaches something inside of me. It tugs at my fucking heart, the icy organ in my chest that's beating frantically like it wants to escape.

"Don't fucking do that again…" She tries to command me, but I don't take her orders. Her chest rising and falling so rapidly it's almost like she's panicking.

"Bring your mouth here, or it's going to be worse." And it will be. I'll fuck her throat while she screams for me to stop if she doesn't do what I tell her to, right now.

Like a good servant, she heeds the warning and scoots back over to me. Obediently she opens her mouth. Her hazel eyes shine with tears as I slip past her lips once more. Fuck, she feels like heaven, but I'll never admit it out loud.

Thrusting deep inside her mouth, I pull back when I hit the back of her throat, and she starts to gag. I decide not to choke her this time. Maybe I've instilled enough fear into her to keep her in line, at least for today.

"Swirl your tongue, and suck," I growl, and fist her hair in my hand. Why I have to tell her this, I don't know. "You should know how to suck a cock good and well by now…"

She whines in protest, her eyes pleading with me, but does as she's told, sucking and licking me like a pro. I knew she'd done this before. I fucking knew it. I don't know why I'm surprised by my own admission. The truth of the kind of person she is was revealed a long time ago. I guess maybe seeing it with my own eyes is shocking.

Refusing to let her ruin a good fucking blow job, I close my eyes and continue to fuck her mouth. Behind my eyes, images of a Harper, I thought I knew, appear. So innocent and sweet. So fucking perfect, it almost hurt. She was mine then. I thought she would be mine forever.

Pleasure builds at the bottom of my spine, a combination of her tongue and the warmth of her mouth catapulting me over the edge. Just as I'm about to come, I still with my cock in her mouth, I open my eyes and watch with carnal need as my sticky seed explodes in her mouth. Tugging her head back, I stare into her angelic face.

"Swallow every fucking drop like a good girl. If you miss

one, I'll make you lick it up off the floor." For a fraction of a second, I think I might be taking this too far. I want to hurt her, break her, but could I degrade her like that? Before I can even think about an answer, she completely surprises the hell out of me when she moans around my cock. She fucking moans while swallowing my come. I don't think a chick has ever fucking done that to me before. The sound vibrates through my entire body, and she sucks the tip drawing out my orgasm a little longer.

Sweet baby Jesus.

I let go of her hair and take a step back, my dick sliding out of her mouth as I do. I have to lean against the vanity behind me as I tuck my dick back in and zip up my pants. Fuck, I don't think I've come so hard from a blow job. In fact, I didn't expect this one to be all that good. Once again, I'm proven wrong. My once upon a time, innocent Harper is anything but innocent. Now she's a sexy siren, probably riding and sucking dick like it's a professional sport.

Composing myself, I look down at Harper kneeling on the floor. Her hands are in her lap, her hair is a sexy mess, and her lips are swollen. Her eyes are still filled with tears, and when our gazes collide, I feel an imaginary boot slam into my gut.

Pain ricochets through my body, and I take an unsteady step back. I already know what's happening here, and I'm not falling for it. Not falling for the innocent fucking act. She isn't innocent. She played me like a fucking fiddle, broke my heart, destroyed my belief in her, and every other woman after her. She ruined me, and now it's time for her to pay the price.

Reaching into my back pocket, I pull out my wallet, "How much do I owe you."

Fire zings across her face, and her hands become tiny clenched fists.

Hit me, baby. I like it rough.

"You're a fucking dick and a crazy asshole. Leave me alone." She starts to push up off the floor, but I laugh and use my hand to push her back down.

"You get up when I say you can get up, not a second sooner." She looks like she might try and fight me on it but doesn't move. I like her like this. Obedient, well-behaved. It almost makes me forget about how she betrayed me.

Almost...

"I hate you," she spits, and I can feel her words as if they're beating against my chest.

Plucking a twenty from my wallet, I toss it at her, and then I lean down into her face. Looking at her bee-stung lips, heart-shaped face, soft, delicate features that would crack underneath the pressure of my hand. *Mark her. Break her.* The beast inside me roars, but I shake off the vicious voice. There will be other chances to hurt her.

Instead, I hammer the final nail into her coffin. "Hate me all you want. But know that I hate you enough for the both of us, and no amount of begging, pleading, or tears will ever change that." And without even waiting for her to respond, I unlock the door and walk out of the bathroom, leaving the door open so the entire hallway can see what we've just done. I have nothing to hide, everyone knows I'm a manwhore, a user of women, but no one knows the reason why. Now Harper can get a taste of my medicine, she can lay in the bed that she's made.

4

HARPER

The door swings open, and Warren walks out, leaving me behind. I'm on my knees, a twenty-dollar bill lying next to me, and I'm pretty sure I still have come on my swollen lips. To make matters worse, a few people look inside, gawking at me like I'm some sideshow.

I get up as fast as I can, tripping over my feet in the process and shut the door, needing a moment to myself. Turning on the faucet, I splash some ice-cold water on my face.

What did I just do? One minute I'm dancing, having a grand time, and the next, I'm on my knees, giving the only guy I've ever loved a blow job. Not to mention my first ever blow job. I shiver, feeling cold all over. He acted like I was supposed to know what I was doing. Why the hell would he think that?

I can still feel his cock at the back of my throat, taste his salty release on my tongue. Was I turned on by what we'd done? A little, okay, more than a little. Mostly though, I just feel empty and used. Tears sting my eyes. I don't want to cry, not really, but the emotions within me are too strong. For years I've wondered what I did wrong, why he never said goodbye, why he changed. After tonight, after I saw the darkness in his eyes, I know whatever it is that made him hate me, it was bad. Horrible. And yet, I can't think of one thing I ever did to him to make him lash out like this at me.

It takes me forever to pull myself together, and I lean against the counter, doing everything I can to gain my composure. A drunk chick stumbles into the bathroom, her eyes are bloodshot and glassy. Her red-stained lips turn into a smirk like she knows something I don't know.

"Could you like, get out?" She slurs and stumbles toward me.

"Gladly," I shove past her and into the hall. The door slams promptly behind me, and then there I am, standing in the middle of a frat house after giving Warren a blow job in the bathroom. I knew I should've fought against Valerie bringing me here. *Stupid.* I'm so stupid. Swiping at my eyes with the back of my hand, I slowly walk down the crowded hall. I make it all of ten feet before a hand clamps down on my shoulder.

Not this again. Without even thinking, I whirl around with my fist clenched, ready to slug Warren right in his stupid jaw. I've had enough for one night. I. Am. Done.

"Whoa, baby..." The guy I don't know sees me with my fist raised and takes a step back. The area is already congested with bodies making it hard to breathe and move.

"Don't call me baby, and don't touch me again," I growl and start to twist back around. Again, my movements are halted when the shit for brains frat boy lunges at me and shoves me into the opposite wall. My back hits first, then my head, bouncing off of it like a ball against the concrete.

"Come on, don't be that way. I saw pretty boy come out of the bathroom there," he points in the direction, "and then I saw you on the floor on your knees. You can't tell me you don't want more thick cock in that pretty mouth of yours." His eyes are glassy, and he smells like a damn distillery. I open my mouth to respond to him, but he takes that moment to swipe his thumb across my bottom lip. I don't even think as I bite the digit, my teeth sinking in his flesh like it's a nice juicy steak.

With a squeal, he pulls his hand back, the lustful gaze he had been giving me seconds ago becomes murderous. "You fucking bitch," he snarls.

"Yeah, I'm a bitch, and when I tell you to leave me alone, maybe listen and actually Leave. Me. Alone." I enunciate each word incase his small brain can't comprehend it.

His gaze narrows and his lips pull into a grim smile. I can feel his gaze on me, and it makes my skin crawl.

"You'll open your mouth for Warren, but you won't for me? You know he doesn't mind sharing his girls."

"I'm not Warren's girl, so you can kindly fuck off." I interrupt, completely dismissing him. All I want to do is find Valerie and escape this fucking hell hole.

He nods, his eyes alone promise a world of pain, though he doesn't take another step toward me, "Okay, I'll be sure to let everyone know who you are...and that when they need a blow job, you're the girl to come to."

"Say whatever you want. I don't care. Just leave me alone." I slip past him and all but run down the hall, refusing to look back and see if he's following me. When I reach the living room, I pull my cell out of my pocket and prepare to dial Valerie's number. My finger hovers over the green call key, but I survey the room one last time and spot her across the living room, sitting on some guy's lap.

Jesus. I can't do this right now. Walking over to her on wobbly legs, I stop dead in my tracks when I find Warren standing there. Smug and confident, he doesn't look like he just got a blow job in the bathroom, he looks like a god. He brings the cup in his hands to his full lips and takes a sip. Everything inside me says to walk away, to leave without talking to Valerie, but I can't. I came with her, so I owe it to her to let her know I'm leaving. Holding my chin high, I take another step, and then another. From this spot, he can oversee the entire room. Almost like he's on his throne merely waiting to lash out at someone who steps out of line.

"Val," I call out to her. She's locked lips with some frat boy, probably one of Warren's friends. Knowing she probably won't hear from the distance I'm at, I walk right over to her and grab her by the arm, tugging her backward. The kiss breaks, and she whirls around, shrugging out of my hold.

"What the hell—"

"Let's go. I want to leave." I don't dare look over at Warren. I can feel his hot gaze on me though, moving over my flesh. Heat blooms in my cheeks, and I try and ignore the feelings forming in my gut. *Ignore him.* I tell myself.

Valerie stares at me for a second before shaking her head, "No. I'm not leaving. I'm having fun, and you should be too."

"Fun?" I snort. "Getting herpes from a frat boy at a party is what you call fun?"

"Whatever, Harper," she rolls her eyes, "Go back to your apartment and cry some more about how alone you are. I'm sure all your friends will care... wait, you don't have any." That's a low blow but not surprising. Valerie is known for saying mean stuff when she drinks, and even meaner stuff when she's around her *friends.*

Sighing, I clench my jaw to stop myself from lashing out at her. Of course, this entire conversation has to happen within ten feet of my biggest bully.

"Yes, Harper, why don't you run along..." Warren's voice

grates on my last nerve. Concentrating on my breathing, I force air in my lungs.

"I'm leaving, Val," I tell her, but all she does is roll her eyes and go back to kissing the guy who has his arms wrapped around her like an octopus.

"Nobody cares," one of the guys standing beside Warren yells as I turn and walk away. When I reach the door and walk outside, I feel a little better. Like I can breathe and think properly.

Wrapping my arms around myself, I walk in the direction of my apartment complex. It's only a couple of blocks away, but it might as well be a thousand miles after everything I've dealt with tonight. Each step I take away from the house, the softer the music gets, and the clearer my thoughts on what happened become.

Holy shit, I gave Warren a blow job. I guess before it hadn't really hit me, but it has now, like a train running into me head-on.

What did I do? Why did I do it, and why the hell did I like it? I search my brain for an answer but find nothing. When it came to Warren and me, we were best friends, but also much more than that. Before my life fell apart and we moved, I was sure that we would marry and live happily ever after. Oh, how wrong I was. Warren wasn't prince charming. He wasn't a knight. He had become what true nightmares were made of. My bully. My monster. My tormentor.

Once upon a time, he had protected me from them. Staring straight ahead, I'm hit right in the chest with a memory from when he was my savior, my all...

How is it that I'd much rather have things thrown at me than be called names? At least, I could clean my clothes, my skin. But words, those couldn't be washed away. They sunk deep into a person's heart.

"Where did you get those shoes, fatty? Goodwill?" Tanya one of my least favorite people ever taunts as I walk into the lunchroom. I can feel her evil eyes against my skin. Without Warren, as my shield, I'm nothing more than a target for everyone's hate. I don't do anything to draw their attention, and I learned a long time ago, there isn't any point in fighting back. I'm a maid's daughter, in a school full of rich assholes.

Keeping my eyes trained on the floor, I make it through the line with my tray of food in hand. Warren was supposed to meet me for lunch, but he's late, so I guess I'll just sit by myself. Peeking up through my lashes, I survey the room. There are students everywhere, which makes me feel a little anxious. I hate being in crowds. Deciding that maybe eating in the bathroom is my best bet, I make a beeline for the double doors that lead out into the hall.

Walking, I keep my eyes trained on my steps, and not on what's going on around me, which is most definitely why I don't notice Griffin until it's too late. The asshole jock slams into me, sending my tray filled with my lunch right into my chest.

"Ooopssss," he snickers, taking a step back. I don't dare look at my shirt because if I do, I know I'll start crying.

"Wrong move, prick," Warren's voice comes out of nowhere, and when I look past Griffin's stocky frame, I spot him. My savior, my white knight. I can breathe a little better, my lungs fill with air at the sight of him. Running across the space separating us, with his fist clenched and his face a mask of fury, he truly does look like a knight. A knight who is about to save his princess...

That wasn't the first time Warren ever hit someone for hurting me. There were many times before that, and after, that he defended my honor. Blinking away the memory, I remind myself that Warren isn't that boy anymore. The one that beat the crap out of a guy for making me wear my lunch.

Lost in thought, I realize how close to my apartment I am. As I walk the rest of the way, this eerie feeling creeps up my spine, the fine hairs on the back of my neck stand on end.

Someone is watching me. Whirling around, my gaze darts over every little thing. The lights in this area are dim and fewer than a couple blocks back, making it difficult to see. Anyone could be hiding in the shadows, though it's probably just Warren following me home, trying to get the upper hand and scare me.

Shaking the feeling away, I hurry the rest of the way to the apartment, picking up speed with each step I take. I'm only a block away when it happens.

Out of nowhere, someone grabs me from behind. With his hands clawing at my upper arms, he drags me into the alley next to my apartment complex. A shrill, piercing scream rips from my lungs, but I might as well do nothing because, in this neighborhood, you can shoot guns, and no one cares.

Panic grips me by the neck and squeezes tightly as my attacker spins me around and pushes me against the cold brick wall. It's dark, and I'm disoriented, my vision blurry with tears. Frantically, I flail my arms around, trying to get this guy away from me.

This is bad. This is so bad. I'm gonna die. I'm gonna die in a horrible way.

"Where the fuck are you going?" Warren's deep voice wraps around my throat, just as he gets a hold of my wrists, halting my movements.

Sucking in a shaky breath, realization sets in...Warren. This is Warren. Even though he has been an ass to me, especially today. I can't help but feel relieved to see him. He was my protector for so long, it's hard not to feel safe with him, no matter how he is acting toward me now.

"Jesus, you scared the shit out of me!" I sob. I hate that I'm crying, but I really thought I was gonna die in this alley. I need to move, find somewhere safer to stay, but I can't afford anything else right now.

"Why the fuck are you here?" His voice is deep, rough, and with his hands still on my arms, I can feel his touch burning through my thin jacket.

"I'm staying with a friend. She lives right over there," I explain, pointing toward my apartment. I don't want him to know where I live, that's the last thing I need right now. In the shadows, it's hard to make out his face, but I can see the flicker of excitement in his gaze. This might be as bad as thinking someone was going to get me after all.

"Why are you following me?"

His lips tip up into a sadistic smile, "Because I'm not done with you. That blow job was nice, but I want more." He takes a step closer, pinning me to the wall with his body, his hard bulge pressing into my stomach. A warmth burns through me. I want him, even though I know I shouldn't. Instantly, I'm reminded of how his cock felt in my mouth, the salty tang of his release, and how wet I was kneeling before him. Warmth gives way to intense cold when I remember how he left me in that bathroom, how he treated me afterward, and how he acted in front of his friends—like I was nothing, no one.

Fuck him. I might be a nobody now, but at some point, I was somebody to him, and that should matter. It should fucking matter. Deep-rooted anger mixes with pain, and it hits me like a freight train, filling me with a newfound strength.

I don't have to do this...deal with him, let him manhandle me like I'm some piece of meat. Taking all that energy, I force it into shoving him away from me. The shove is hard, but it only moves him an inch. Cold tears streak my cheeks as I stand on shaky legs, partially leaning against the brick wall.

I hate how weak I am right now. How broken I feel because of him. Looking up, I see Warren's face is a mixture of shock and something else, something deeper. I don't bother to internalize that look. All I want is for him to go away.

"Don't ever fucking touch me again!" I yell, my voice dripping with hurt and disappointment. I'm so disappointed in him, but more so in myself. At what we've become. How did we get here? What did I do to make him hate me so much?

I almost sigh in relief when his arms fall down to his sides, and even in the dim light, I can make out his facial expression, and see that he is feeling the same way. Taking that chance to escape, I push past him and run the last block to my place, only stopping when I've made it inside. Slamming the door behind me, I lock the deadbolt and slide down the door, trying to catch my breath.

I sink my fingers into my hair and try and drown out the throbbing forming behind my eyes. Tonight, I made a mistake, one that I won't make again. Warren got the best of me, in more than one way, but next time, he won't. Next time, I'll be ready.

5

WARREN

I drop the weights at my feet and blow out a harsh breath. My muscles burn, and sweat drips down my back and forehead, but I feel lighter and more at ease now. Shaking out my limbs, I contemplate running on the treadmill to tire myself out.

Lately, all I've been able to do is work out. The idea of having sex with another chick... it makes me feel nauseous. It also makes me angry as hell because that means Harper is sinking her little claws into my skin and worming her way into my brain.

My best prick of a friend drops his own weights, and I can feel him watching me.

"What the fuck?" I growl.

"You've been acting weird. Is something going on?" Parker asks, "Anything you want to talk about?" He sits down on one of the nearby benches. Who is he? Doctor Phil? He gets a girlfriend, and suddenly he's grown a heart? Yeah, no. I don't want to talk about all the fucked up feelings that are barely contained beneath my skin.

"Nothing is going on, just been stressed. You know how my dad gets about my grades and keeping up appearances." I shove a hand through my sweaty mop of hair. I'm not lying, not really. My dad does ride my ass about my grades. Keeping up appearances? Not so much.

Parker tilts his head to the side, "Right..." He scoffs. "You know you can't lie to me. I know you too well. Out with it, who pissed in your cheerios?"

"No one," I can feel the frustration that I just burned off, building again. Like a steaming pot, I'm close to boiling over all over again.

"Dude, that chick from the party..." Easton comes walking over to us. The guy can be a total douchebag, and he's a bigger asshole than even I am, and that speaks volumes.

"What girl?" I ask, entertaining the idea of a conversation. Anything is better than being forced to spill my guts to Parker.

"Yeah, what girl?" Parker perks up his interest in the subject, annoying me further.

Easton rolls his eyes, "The chick that gave you a bj in the bathroom. The hooker." He's looking at me like I'm an idiot, and I'm half-tempted to punch him in his stupid face. Then I realized what he just called Harper, and I clench my hand into a fist, my teeth grinding so hard I swear they're seconds away from shattering.

"What did you just call her?" I seethe, not even attempting to hide my anger.

"The hooker. What's her name? Hannah or Harper?" His brow furrows in confusion, probably not understanding why I'm reacting the way I am. *Well, I don't understand either.*

I don't care about girls. They're nice to look at and to fuck, but that's as far as my feelings go for them. I use them as a place to put my dick, so why the fuck am I getting territorial and pissed over someone calling Harper a whore?

Because she's yours, and nobody fucks with what's yours. A voice inside my head says. Easton continues without question, "Apparently, after you walked out of the bathroom, James walked in. She asked him if he wanted a blow job, and James being James, said yeah. She sucked him off right there. He said it was the best blow job he's ever had for twenty bucks." He laughs like it's so funny.

"I'm pretty sure I saw this chick working the pole across town. I swear I've seen her there, at the Night Shift. So, next time I'm there, I'm going to see what a twenty can get me."

I don't know what sets me off then. Like a wildfire spreading out of control, I lash out. Grabbing Easton by the throat, I shove him against the wall, my lip curls back, and I can feel the dark venom filling my veins. Even if she isn't mine, she won't be anyone else's either. I'll be the one to break her, to hurt her, to make her bleed.

"Don't even think about touching her. She's mine..." I basically spit the words at him before I can stop myself. *Mine?* She's not mine. She's not anything, just some stupid girl I had a crush on when we were kids. His gaze widens before it simply turns into confusion. Fuck, I'm confused myself.

Releasing him with a shove, knowing that this is not his fault. It's hers, it's all her fault. I whirl around and grab my towel off the bench beside Parker. I'm beyond agitated now, enraged even. I knew she slept around, did shit with other guys, but I guess knowing about it and hearing it are two different things.

"What the fuck was that?" Parker's voice meets my ears, and I feel him trailing behind me as I exit the weight room.

"Don't make it into something more than it is, and it won't

be anything," I answer without turning around. I need to go back to my apartment and change, but more than that, I need to talk to Harper. She's the reason for this burning rage... and she needs to be the one I dispense it on. Her appearing back in my life is causing mass chaos, and I need to end this, get her the fuck away before something bad happens.

"Dude!" He grabs onto my shoulder, pulling me backward at the same time. I spin around, ready to punch one of my best friends in the face. Like a fly that won't go away, he just keeps annoying me.

"I said to fucking leave it." My nostrils flare... I'm going to explode, shatter and all because of that brown hair, hazel-eyed girl.

Parker's gaze flicks from my face and down to my fists and back up again. He's not scared. He can take a punch or five, but that's not the point. I don't want to punch him. I want to ignore these feelings. This anger and madness.

"You've never stuck up for a girl. You've also never looked at me like you are right now, so unless you want to throw down, I suggest you tell me what the fuck is going on?"

"I'm not in the mood for this." I shrug his hand off. "And I don't want to fight with you. Just leave it alone." I do my best to remain calm, but all the perfect ingredients for a storm are brewing inside of me, and I know it will soon be unleashed, bringing down everything in my path.

Parker shakes his head, "Sure, just ignore it. Seems like it's working well for you."

"I don't want to talk about her. Not with you or anyone else."

"Who is she? Is she that girl from the lunchroom? The one you looked like you could kill with a single glance?" I forgot about that day. He had seen her too and even asked about her.

I told him she was a ghost, and that's exactly what she is. A ghost that haunts my every thought.

Leaning into his face, so I can prove a point, I sneer, "She is no one. Now. Leave. It. Alone. I'm not you Parker. I won't ever fall at my knees for her like you did Willow. What she did to me, there is no coming back from that."

Something flickers in Parker's eyes, his jaw tightens, and he takes a step back.

"Okay, if you don't want to talk about it, then whatever…"

I damn near sigh in relief. Any more talk about Harper and my brain might explode. It's bad enough that she's everywhere I look. I don't have to torment myself further by saying her name out loud.

"Let's get some grub. I'm fucking starving." I let the tension ease out of me.

"Okay, let me text Willow and tell her we're going to lunch." Parker pulls out his cell. I roll my eyes, but I understand. I'm happy for him. He found love and happiness after all the darkness. Too bad my story won't end the same.

After what I heard about Harper earlier, I think it's time I shake things up a bit. I think it's time that I make it known that she's mine to take from, mine to fuck, mine to hurt and break.

∽

IT TAKES A SHIT-TON OF PATIENCE, but I somehow manage to keep myself busy waiting for Harper to be released from her last class. I can't help but check her out as she slips from the auditorium and down the long hall toward the double doors that lead outside.

I could have asked Parker to figure out what dorms Harper lives in, but he has been bothering me enough about her. So,

I'm doing the next best thing... following her like a creep. Making sure I stay far enough behind her not to seem suspicious, I walk with her, never taking my eyes off of her.

Surprisingly, she passes all the dorms and starts to walk off the campus. As soon as I realize she is walking in the direction of the neighborhood, I caught her in the other night, my irritation grows. She said she was staying with a girlfriend, but I had my doubts right away. Does she have a boyfriend here? If she does, I'll kill him, then I'll fuck her right in front of his body just to drive the point home.

With every step I take, the anger in my gut festers. I can't stop thinking about her having a boyfriend or even a fuck buddy. My lip curls all on its own, my body vibrating with energy.

We walk for about fifteen minutes before we make it to the same building I saw her run into the other night. She unlocks the front door and slips inside. Bolting forward, I grip onto the edge of the door before it can close all the way. Startled by my presence, she twists around with her fist raised up in the air, her gaze hard.

Pushing inside, I snicker, "Who are you gonna hurt with those?"

"Seriously, Warren? Didn't I tell you to leave me alone?" Turning away from me, she starts walking up the stairs, her feet stomping on each step. Letting my gaze wander, I can see that the whole place is falling apart, and Jesus fucking Christ, it smells like a urinal in here. How does anyone live here? I feel dirty just stepping in this place.

"Good thing I don't care what you want." I follow her without another word. I need to see where she is going and who the fuck she is staying with. The impulse is too strong. I want to know everything, but especially why the fuck she is staying here when she has a scholarship and should be in the dorms.

"Go away, Warren. I'm not letting you inside." Our eyes lock as she looks at me over her shoulder. Is this the part where I leave? Because if so, she's sorely mistaken. Stopping at a door on the left side, she fumbles with the key. Obviously, she's distracted.

Staring up at the ceiling, I direct my attention back to her when she finally gets it to go inside the lock and turns it. As soon as she pushes the door open, I spring forward, wrapping an arm around her waist, and carrying her into the room.

"You didn't really think that would get rid of me?" I ask with a grin. Yes, I know I'm an asshole, but I have my reasons just as any asshole does. She skirts away from me, and I shut the door, closing us inside together. Alone at last.

"I was hoping it would." She huffs, switching on the light.

Taking in the tiny apartment, if you can even call it that, it's more like a small room, barely enough space to hold a twin-size bed, a kitchenette, a table and chair. Harper throws her bag down next to the bed and peels her jacket off. And then it hits me like a kick to the ball sack. *She* lives here. This is her fucking apartment. There is no *friend*, no boyfriend either, or fuckboy, at least not in sight.

"You lied to me. You said you were staying with a friend." I pin her with an accusing glare.

She rolls her pretty hazel eyes, "I didn't want you to know where I live. Well, now, you know. Congratulations. Sorry, it's not up to your standards. There are no butlers, or maids, no chefs, and the bed doesn't have Egyptian cotton sheets." No, there definitely isn't any of that here. This looks like a room that a whore would use to sell herself out of.

"Actually, my standards are pretty low. I'm here with you, aren't I?"

"Whenever you're done with your insults, you can go ahead and leave, doors over there in case you can't pull your head out of your ass and find it."

Good one. Ignoring what she said because I don't really care what she has to say, I get straight to the point. The real reason I came here.

Taking a step toward her, I let myself turn into the predator. "Heard you sucked off someone else at the party. James, I believe. That's going to stop. If you have to stay at this school, the only cock you're going to suck, ride, or choke on will be mine."

"Of course, someone saw what happened." She shakes her head, her eyes colliding with mine. Fire sparks between us, zinging through the air. "I did not and will not fuck anyone else, and above all you!" Her words slice through me like a dull knife, and before I know what I'm doing, I close the distance between us in one large stride. I'm like a caged monster that's been freed. My hand flies up, and my fingers wrap around her delicate throat. Fragile, so fragile, like glass. Pushing her back until she falls onto the bed, I climb on top of her.

"You spread your legs for who knows who, but not for me?" With my free hand, I start to undo her blouse. The heat of her skin beckons me forward. She's a beacon of light in my dark mind, and I want to dull out her light. Trying with little effect, she slaps me away, but that just makes me tighten my grip on her throat.

Careful... I tell myself, my eyes piercing hers. The blackness bleeds out of me, filling the room to the point of suffocation. I can't breathe. All I can do is feel. Feel the pain, the sadness, the anger. That's what seeing her does to me. It brings out the worst in me.

"Don't," she pleads, and I try to ignore the panic in her voice, but it calls to me. I want to hear her cries, of want, of fear.

An inch from her face, I snarl, "Don't what? Hurt you? Break your heart like you broke mine?" Her eyes widen at my words, confusion reflecting in them like she doesn't understand what I'm saying, or why I'm acting like this. Surely, she doesn't think that I forgot her secret? She opens her mouth to say something, but I don't let her. I can't listen to another lie coming out of her mouth.

Easing back, I let my eyes roam down over her perfect body. She still looks so innocent; she still looks like *my* Harper, and that only makes all of this so much worse.

All over again, she's here in front of me but somehow lost forever. I'm so fucking furious, I feel like I'm going to burst if I don't let this out. Anger overwhelms me, overriding all reasoning, and I let go of her throat, knowing that I'll squeeze too hard and cut off her air supply if I don't. I want to hurt her, not kill her.

Balling my hand into a fist, I rear back and punch the mattress beside her head. I don't know what's happening to me. The rage burns, it owns me. Harper covers her face, protecting it like I'm going to hit her, and that only infuriates me more.

Getting off of her, I turn and punch the closest wall. Pain shoots through my hand and up my arm as it makes contact with the old plaster wall. I welcome the pain. I hold on to that physical pain because it hurts less than the kind of pain she causes me. Taking a deep breath, I compose myself enough to speak.

"You need to shut up, or this is going to end badly for both of us. Your voice makes me lose my fucking mind, and I want to hurt you, not kill you, so please shut up."

Her body trembles on the bed, and I take another calming breath. *One. Two. Three.* I count back to myself because counting and breathing are the only two things saving us right now.

"I heard you've been dancing at the local strip club, so why don't you give me a little show to calm me down?"

Harper eases into a sitting position, and I look over at her. She looks as if she's afraid, but not afraid enough. There is fire in her, and I'm going to do everything in my power to extinguish it.

"If you're implying that I'm a stripper, then you're going to need to go back to whoever told you that lie and tell them they're an idiot. I would never strip for money. I have morals, no offense to the girls that do it, but..."

Rubbing at my temples with two fingers, I snap, "Get up, take off your fucking clothes and start dancing. Otherwise, I'll do it for you."

Gritting her teeth, I can see the defiance pooling in her eyes. She lifts her chin, holding it high as she pushes up off the bed. Come on, baby, walk over here and tell me to fuck off, I dare you. Though she's nearly a foot shorter than me, she stands tall like a flower in a field of weeds.

"I'm gonna tell you the same thing I told your friend at the party... fuck off and leave me alone!" She raises her voice, and all I can do is smile.

"Wrong answer," I growl as I place my knee on the bed. Like a frightened child, she scurries away from me and toward the wall. Dumb girl. She can't escape me... not now that she's here. I grab her leg, so she can't get far. This time, when I look into her face, I see fear, real fear. A look she has never given me before. For the first time tonight, my anger lessens, not by a lot thought and not enough to let go of her.

"Can you please just leave," she begs, her voice trembling.

I try a different tactic. I shouldn't give a fuck about her living situating, but stupidly I do.

"Why do you live here? Aren't you on a scholarship?" I want to know everything about her, every little detail. Where she went? How she ended up back here? Who she let fuck her?

"Yes," she bites at her bottom lip nervously, and then it clicks.

"Aren't you supposed to stay in the dorms? Doesn't the scholarship cover on-campus housing?" I don't know shit about this kind of stuff, but I can easily find out.

"I can't afford the dorms," is all she says, her eyes dropping to the floor.

"Don't make enough money at the strip club?" I lift a questioning brow.

"I'm not a stripper! Jesus." She growls, her claws finally coming out again. I like her fragile, and purring with fear, but I also like her fierce, willing to fight me tooth and nail. It's a contradiction, and I can't explain it. I know it's wrong, but I love this push and pull. I feed off of it like a parasite.

"Okay, so what will fifty dollars get me?"

Her tiny little jaw tightens, and in a flash, her hand is making contact with my face. I feel the sting, my head turning to the side with the force of the hit.

Fuck...me... The copper tang of blood fills my mouth. If she were anyone else, I'd hit her back, but she isn't just anyone. She's Harper. *My* Harper. And I've got something better up my sleeve.

6

HARPER

It feels like I'm having a heart attack, and my lungs are collapsing at the same time. Why didn't I think before I slapped him? His pupils are blown, his eyes almost black, feral.

"Strip, now. If you don't, it won't be pretty...and I don't want to be responsible for breaking you, not yet at least." The darkness inside of him pours out, terrifying me into a shocked stupor. Every single bone in my body says to run, escape, my fight or flight instincts kick in full force, but if I give way to running, he'll chase, and when he catches me...

"You won't hurt me," I say, my voice small even though I try to sound strong and determined.

"Are you sure about that?"

I nod, even though I'm not sure at all.

"Maybe not, but I can make your life hell in other ways. I know people at the school. I can get your grades dropped; make you lose your precious scholarship."

Shit, that I believe. He could fuck this up for me. Something I worked so hard for. This scholarship means everything to my family and me. I won't ever get a chance like this again. A chance for a better life.

Shivering, I swallow down my fear and stop myself from thinking on it any further. I can do this. I can do what he wants so he'll leave me alone. With shaking hands, I reach for my shirt, lifting the hem, I pull it up and over my head. The cold air of the room makes contact with my skin, and I consider tugging the thing back down, but the way Warren is looking at me now, tells me he has very little patience left.

Next is the button on my jeans. I flick it, listening as the pop resonates through the room, then I slide them down my legs slowly, telling myself, he's not really here, and I'm just wearing a bikini. Tears prick my eyes as I stand before him in my underwear, my body on display to him. A boy I used to think was my everything, my knight, until he turned into the cruel monster that he is today.

"You didn't think it was going to be that easy, did you?" A vicious grin that could only be described as Satan smiling at you, graces his lips.

"What do you mean?" I ask, confused while doing my best not to give away how afraid of him and this situation I am. There is no reasoning with Warren, no understanding him. It's clear he wants something from me or at least wants me to pay for something I've done, but what is that something? A question pricks my tongue, and just as I'm about to give voice to my thoughts, he clears his throat.

"Bra and panties off. Then, I want you to go over to the bed, crawling on your hands and knees. Lie on your back and close your eyes."

Shaking like a leaf in the summer breeze, I chew on my lip, "Warren..."

"Do it," he growls. That lean but athletic body of his

vibrates with uncontrolled chaos, and I know if I object, all hell will break loose. Part of me wants to see him lose control while the other is scared of it.

Right now, I think the scared part wins, so tucking my tail between my legs, I slip my fingers into the side of my panties and shove them down, watching as they fall to the floor.

Without looking up, I unsnap my bra and toss it down as well. Then like a dog, I drop to my knees, the coldness of the floor against my skin makes me wince, but I bite the inside of my cheek to hide the sound. I refuse to give him any more leverage, to let him know how scared I am.

Crawling across the floor, I can feel his eyes on me. As wrong as it is, and as slimy as I feel about it, my insides clench at the uncertainty of what may happen. My core pulses with need, and I want to tell my stupid hormones to go away, that they don't understand the person they're reacting to is fucked up and crazy.

Reaching the bed, I pause, can I really do this? Can I swallow my pride and let him use my body just to keep him happy and keep my scholarship safe?

"Don't tempt me, Harper. Please don't fucking tempt me." Warren's voice is cold and downright sinister. A chill of terror blankets my body, and I obey him. Crawling up onto the mattress, I lie down on my back. Exhaling a ragged breath, I close my eyes and say a silent prayer. When I hear his footsteps echoing off the floor, I start to shake.

What sick and twisted thing is he going to do?

"I used to think the world of you, Harper, that you were it for me. That you were this perfect little thing..." His fingers trail over my skin, and I flinch, wanting to open my eyes and see what he's doing.

"I don't understand..." I respond without thinking.

"Shhh, I didn't tell you to speak," Warren whispers, and I can feel his hot breath against my face. A second later, I feel him pushing my thighs apart. My body hums, heat pulses in my pussy, and radiates outward. *This is wrong.* You don't want him, I want to scream to my body, but it's already betrayed me.

"Spread your thighs and keep them spread. You don't want to know what happens if you don't." I don't need him to tell me. The warning is clear enough. Trailing his fingers down between my breasts, I wait with bated breath for his next move. I'm completely exposed, a fallen angel lying at the devil's feet.

Rolling my nipple between two fingers, he causes both pain and pleasure to zing through me. I inhale sharply, and whimper as he releases my breast and does the same to the other.

"You're a filthy fucking girl, and even though you've been bad and definitely don't deserve my tongue, I'm going to give it to you. I'm going to show you what you could've fucking had..." I let my eyes flutter open just in time to see him dropping to his knees before me. His fingers bite into my ass as he lifts me, bringing my pussy to his mouth as if I'm a steak and he hasn't eaten in months.

At the first touch of his tongue against my clit, I whimper. At the second touch, I squirm, and by the third lick, I'm fighting for breath. The man is starving, feasting on me, and no matter how wrong this is, I don't want him to stop.

Sucking on the tiny bundle of nerves, he makes my body hum and my head spin. I can't comprehend what is up or down with his tongue against my pussy.

"So delicious...almost sweet," he growls against my wet folds, and I swear his voice could be as good as *Roger* my vibrator.

"Oh... Oh..." I fist the sheets, thrashing against them like a helpless animal that's being sacrificed.

His tongue starts to move faster, flicking my clit hard, and I bite my bottom lip to stop the scream that threatens to escape. Oh, fuck. I'm coming. I can feel it pulsing, building up, the pressure becoming too much.

"Warren..." I scream his name as I fall apart. Light flashes before my eyes and my hips lift. I feel nothing and everything all at once. There is a buzzing in my ears, and as I drift down from my high, I find Warren is no longer between my legs but standing. The juices of my release coat his lips, and this strange, twisted part of me wants to kiss him. To taste myself on his lips.

"Keep your legs fucking closed. Your pussy is mine to eat, fuck, and play with, no one else better touch you. I'll kill them and make you watch."

He can't be serious, but judging by the look in his eyes, he is. My gaze drifts down to his crotch, a significant bulge remains there. I wonder if he's going to find some girl to suck him off or go back to wherever it is he stays and fuck some random chick. The thought hurts me more than I want to admit.

"Until next time," he smiles and walks to the door. Once he's gone, I remain on the bed, staring up at the ceiling. There are a thousand emotions lying dormant inside me, a million thoughts swirling, but all I can think about is... why does he hate me so much? What did I do to him?

∽

FLIPPING the page of the textbook, I try my best to follow what professor Brice is saying. I've always been good in school, straight A student and all. I got here on an academic scholarship after all, but with everything going on, my mind is just too busy to concentrate on school. It's like I'm developing a form of ADHD which I've never had in my life.

Warren hasn't only gotten under my skin, he has weaseled his way into every part of my life, my every thought, even my dreams at night. There is no escaping him, which was his plan all along.

"Hey," the guy sitting two seats down from me calls, trying to get my attention. He's been staring at me for the better part of an hour, but even that is easily forgotten with Warren invading my mind. I pin the scrawny guy with a glare, wondering what the hell he wants from me. Doesn't my face say it enough: don't talk to me.

"What?" I ask in a harsher tone than necessary.

"Aren't you, Harper?"

"Yeah, that's my name. Do I know you?"

Leaning in a little closer so no one else can hear, he asks, "No, but James told me what you do... that ah, you know... for twenty dollars."

Huh? It takes me a moment to let his words sink in and understand who and what he is talking about. *James?* He must be the guy from the party, and true to his word, he is spreading rumors about me. Great, that explains why Warren told me to keep my legs closed. He probably heard the same rumor and assumes the worst. *Of course, he does...*

"Listen, the truth is James asked me to suck him off. I agreed, you know just for fun, not for money because I'm not a whore. But when he got his dick out, it was just so small, I couldn't help but laugh. Like, seriously, it was the tiniest dick I've ever seen. Probably considered a micro-penis." The guy's mouth pops open, shock riddling his features. "So that's why he started the rumor about me giving him a blow job for cash because he's just mad and embarrassed that he has such a small penis, and I laughed."

"Well, I don't have a small penis. So, will you give me a blow job? You know, just for fun?" His cheeks redden, and I can tell this isn't something he does often. Nonetheless, he's being a douchebag by asking me to suck his dick as if this is a damn service I'm running.

"No," I snap, and return my eyes back to my book.

What an ass.

Ten minutes later, Professor Brice dismisses the class, and I quickly gather my stuff and shove it in my backpack. Without looking at the guy again, I scurry out of the room and down the hall. Thank god this was my last class for the day because I can't wait to get home and just relax. There are way too many things on my mind right now.

My walk to the apartment is short and uninterrupted, and I use the time to try and clear my head. The clearing of my head was pointless though, because as soon as I walk up to my apartment door, I immediately know that something is wrong.

I know for a fact that I locked my door this morning. I always double and triple check to make sure the doors are locked. You can never be too sure in this neighborhood. Taking in that the door is cracked open a few inches, I know someone broke in.

Like the idiot I am, I don't call the cops or think about calling anyone at all because let's be honest, who would care anyway? Taking a cautious step forward, I push the door open and peer into my tiny apartment.

My heart is racing in my chest so hard it feels like it's trying to escape. I take a couple calming breaths in an attempt to get my breathing under control and in turn, my heart rate.

Stay calm. I tell myself and try and rationalize the situation. Who would break into my apartment? Don't they know I don't own anything of importance?

Holding my breath, I listen for any noise, maybe the intruder is still here. Panic seizes me, and I almost take a step back out of instinct. *No.* This is my home. This is all I have. Calming myself once more and after a short while of not hearing anything, I step closer, crossing the threshold and stepping into the room.

Like a detective, my eyes scan the room for any details. The books on my small bookshelf above the bed have been knocked down, the bed that was made up this morning is disheveled, and the drawers of my dresser are all opened with the contents poured out on the floor. It doesn't look like anything is missing, but like someone went through all my stuff. Shutting the door behind me, I close myself inside the room.

Who would want to hurt me?

Warren. Of course, he would do something like this. Ever since my first day here, he's tried to scare me into leaving. I'll bet this was nothing more than another tactic to get me to leave. Ha, jokes on him. I'm not going anywhere. I wasn't before, but I'm definitely not now.

7

WARREN

"What do you need this info for anyway?" Damon questions, curiously. His mom works in the administration office, so I had him go in and get all the info on Harper for me. It would've been easier had I asked Parker, but that would mean talking to him about Harper, and I'm not ready to do that yet.

"Don't ask questions, just give me the fucking papers I asked for." He hands me the papers, and I snatch them from his hand, almost ripping them. Right then and there, I start to read over the information. I'm only a couple sentences in when I realize Damon is still standing there, his eyes trained on me.

"What?" I bark, on the verge of losing my temper.

"I was just wondering who she was? I know her name is Harper, but..." The rest of the words never get a chance to pass his lips because my hand wraps around his throat, cutting off his words and air. When it comes to Harper, I'll hurt anyone I have to. The only person that is going to own her, or hurt her, is me.

Getting right in his face, I snarl, "Don't fucking say her name. Don't even think about her. Forget I even had you do this for me because if you don't, I'll make you forget."

Damon's eyes bulge out of his face, and he somehow manages to nod his head. Releasing him with a shove that sends him staggering backward, I fist the paper in my other hand and turn and start walking away. Once I reach the mess hall, I lean against the cold brick and uncrumple the paper. As I read over the information, a smile forms on my lips.

This is the exact ammunition I needed to trap her and keep her right where I want. By living off-campus, she's violating her scholarship. According to this paper, she gets money specifically for campus housing, but she has been misusing those funds, living in that shitty apartment instead... Oh, things aren't looking good for my girl.

My girl. I scoff at the thought. She is mine, but she isn't a girl, she is all woman now. I wonder how she'll react when I tell her that I know her secret.

Grabbing my phone out of my pocket, I pull up her class schedule. She is about to get off for the rest of the day. I have another late class, but I can skip it and still manage to pass. I'm already getting A.

Shoving my phone back in my pocket, I walk across campus to the science lab. I'm barely around the corner in the hallway, when I hear Harper's voice echo through the hall. She is standing right outside of class, Easton is with her. His back is to me, but I know it's him from his coat, hair, and the way he carries himself. They are talking, then he says something to make her laugh.

Jealousy burns through me like a hot iron. I'm a few feet in front of them when Harper looks up, her eyes meet mine, and instantly her smile fades away, a deep frown appearing instead. Easton turns and sees me coming, he nods, but then takes in my angry face. The fucker has the audacity to roll his eyes at me. Shaking his head, he takes a step away from her.

"Don't get your panties in a bunch, Warren. We're just talking about class," Easton says when I'm close enough. Easton better be glad he's my friend and roommate, otherwise, I'd rip him apart like a dog protecting its bone.

Giving him a bored expression, I say, "Didn't I tell you not to talk to her at all? I know you, Easton. I know you don't *just* talk to a girl."

"God, first Parker, now you," he shakes his head. "What is this world coming to?"

Ignoring his stupid comment, I wrap my fingers around Harper's wrist and pull her away from Easton and down the hall with me. To my utter shock, she follows me without a word, that is, until we are outside and away from any listening ears. Then with a tug, she pulls her arm out of my grip.

"What the hell is wrong with you? I'm seriously starting to think you need some medical attention. First, you follow me, stalk me, and humiliate me. Then you break into my apartment, destroying the place, and now you won't even let me talk to people? I'm done with your mind games, Warren."

Out of everything that she says, the only thing I pick up on is that she says someone has broken into her apartment. Seeing red, I grab her by the chin, watching as she winces and tries to pull from my hold.

"Did you just say someone broke into your place?" The rational part of me says who cares, but the part of me that owns her, screams *mine*. If someone is breaking into her apartment, that means they're trying to take what is mine, and no fucking way is that happening.

Breaking out of my hold, Harper staggers back, anger

pooling in her hazel depths, "Don't play stupid. I know it was you. You're the only one that would try and hurt me."

I tip my head back, and a humorless laugh escapes, "How would me coming to your apartment when you're not there benefit me? Plus, let's be real. To get in your apartment, I wouldn't have to break-in. I'd just knock on the door, and you'd let me in."

"You're mental and should definitely be institutionalized. I know you want me to leave, but what you are doing now is kind of mental. To break-in, and go through my stuff, don't you think that's unhinged at all?"

I give her a second to gather her wits, but then she starts spouting off again, "I mean, of course, you wouldn't think that because you did it," she snarls the last few words.

Having had enough of being accused of something I definitely didn't do. I grab her by the waist and pull her to my body. My heart beats heavy in my chest when her hands press against it. It feels like forever since I kissed her lips, ones I want to bite and fuck again.

Whispering against her skin, "I didn't fucking break into your apartment. I'm fucking crazy, yes, but I'm not stupid. I don't do stuff unless it benefits me, and this definitely doesn't."

Harper's gaze widens at my confession, and I practically see her pulse jump in her throat. Slowly, she pieces the puzzle together, "But if... If you didn't, then..."

I nod. "That's right if it wasn't me, then someone else did... Which means you won't be staying in that shithole anymore."

"You don't get to decide where I stay," she snaps, trying to step away from me, but I'm faster and stronger. Grabbing her by the hip, I pick her up and toss her over my shoulder like a rag doll. As soon as she realizes what's happening, her mouth starts running. "Are you fucking kidding me? Let me down!"

Her small fists pound against my back, but they don't hurt. It's cute that she thinks hitting me will make me put her down.

"Stop your bellyaching. I'm basically doing you a favor. Think of it like the golden days, when I let you and your parents stay in the mansion with us."

"I hate you. I hate you so much." She seethes, continuing to beat against my back with a furious rage. "This is kidnapping!" I carry her with ease to the car, never missing a beat. My dick gets hard as I cop a feel of her ass cheek, which is right next to my face. Plump, and perfect for slapping... I want to bury my face in between her creamy thighs again. Lick her from one hole to the other and then fuck her in both.

Shit, I'm getting carried away.

I don't put her down until we get to my car, and when she's back on her feet, I keep a firm hold of her arm. I don't feel like chasing her through the parking lot right now, and I know that as soon as I release her, she's going to run.

"Get in on your own, or I'll make you get in. The choice is yours."

"Fuck you, Warren! None of this is my choice! You're a monster, a cruel, horrible monster," she yells while struggling to break free.

"Keep preaching your dislike, but no one is listening, sweetheart." Opening the door with my free hand, I push her in with the other. Like I expected, she digs her feet in, fighting back against me, but she fails to understand something. I don't give a fuck what I have to do to get her in this car. She's getting in. Giving her a hard shove, she ducks her head at the last second before hitting the seat.

"Now, be a good girl and stay inside, or you can kiss your scholarship goodbye. I don't think the school would approve if they knew you are staying off-campus." That gets her attention. She looks up at me with a different kind of panic in her eyes now. "Yeah, that's right, I know about the money that's supposed to go to on-campus housing."

"Warren..." The way she says my name, with so much helplessness, it makes my insides twist. She did this to us. She broke us. She ruined what we had. I can't feel bad for her. Not when I gave her a chance. Not when I told her what would happen if she didn't leave.

Defeated, she places her hands in her lap and lowers her chin to her chest. I shut the door and quickly walk around, climbing into the driver's seat. I start the car and the hum of the engine filters into the car.

Backing out of the parking lot, I head toward my condo, which is only a couple blocks away. Harper moves as far away from me as she can, plastering herself to the car door.

"Where are we going?" she questions, her voice quiet.

Turning onto the street, I answer, "Not to your shithole, that's for sure."

"You can't just make people go places with you. It's against the law, and crazy..."

"You say that, but yet, here you are, in my car, headed to my place with me." I grin and punch the gas.

"Whatever is going on in that sick mind of yours, just do it already. I want to get it over with, so I can go on with my life without you." *Like you did before.*

"And ruin being able to have you do whatever I want, whenever I want?" I shake my head. "Yeah, I don't think so. I think I'll use you until I'm done and tired of you. Then I'll toss you to the vultures."

A few minutes later, we pull into the driveway of the condo I share with Cameron and Easton. Harper doesn't even blink when she sees the place. It's far bigger than three college guys need, but it's what we wanted, and since we can afford it, I don't see the harm. I mean, what the hell else are we supposed to spend our parents' money on?

"I'm not staying here." Harper crosses her arms over her chest and stares out the window.

Grinning, I lean across the center console, and kill the engine at the same time, "You are because if you refuse, you're fucked. If you don't listen to me, or do whatever I tell you, you're fucked too. Well, you're fucked either way, literally and figuratively, but this is your best bet, so just go with it."

"I am not having sex with you, and I'm not getting out of this car."

"You really want to play this game?" I challenge.

"It's not a game, this is my life. My body. I'm not a doll, you can't just do whatever you want with me."

"But I can..." I get out of the car and walk around. Harper gets out before I make it to her door, and I grab her wrist before she can try and make a run for it. "I'll tell you what, you behave in there, and I'll let you sleep in my bed with me tonight."

Harper snorts, "What makes you think that I would want that?"

"It's either with me, or I'll make you sleep with Cameron or Easton. You know Easton, of course, seemed like you fancy him. Maybe you'd like them both at the same time? They're my roommates." For a split second, I think I just made a mistake saying this. If she tells me she would rather sleep with one of them, then I'll probably end up killing someone tonight. No way in fucking hell is one of those douchebags touching her.

To my relief, she doesn't seem too keen at the thought. In fact, she looks a little nervous about the idea. "I definitely won't sleep with them either. How about I sleep on the couch?"

"How about... no?" I tell her and start walking her inside. Easton is still at school, but I think Cameron is here, which I dislike greatly. For the first time since moving here, I wish I lived alone. Not that I think either of them is stupid enough to try something.

They know better.

Dragging her into the house, I close the door behind us. Voices filter into the foyer. I can make out the voice of a girl, and the grunts must be Cameron's. What the fuck, I told him no more fucking on the couch.

"Oh, Cameron," some chick moans, and I stop midstep, my gaze shooting to Harper. Her eyes grow wide, and her cheeks turn a soft pink.

"Is he..." her words cut off, and I grin because anything that makes her uncomfortable is a win in my book.

"Fucking a chick in the open...yes. Want to join them? Cam loves to share. Him and Easton share all the time." It feels like I'm swallowing rocks as I say the words. Cam might share, but I don't.

"No," Harper says like I just asked her the most outrageous thing. Why does she have to act so damn innocent all the time? It enrages me and turns me on at the same time. I know she's already fucked a shit-ton of guys, so she needs to quit with the act. Then again, I doubt any of them could ever amount to what it will be like for her to be with me.

"Boo. Since you aren't interested in a threesome, we should probably go," I turn down the long hall to my left, dragging her every step of the way. When I reach my door, I turn to her. "This is where the magic happens."

She doesn't laugh or smile. In fact, she gives me a bored

expression. Oh lord, we can't have that. Wouldn't want her getting bored on me.

Opening the door, I tug her inside and then release her, before closing and locking the door behind us. Maybe I should feed her, or something. At the thought, I wonder if she's been eating well? Does she even have enough money for food? She's getting money for housing, so she must be using it somehow. Maybe that's all the money she has unless Easton was right, and she works at the strip club.

I start to strip out of my clothes, pulling my shirt off and tossing it onto the floor. Harper crosses her arms over her chest, the movement drawing my attention to her tits. Fuck, I can't wait to see them again.

"I'm not having sex with you, so if that's what you're planning to do, then just know it will be rape. I will never sleep with you." She raises her chin up, and the defiance in her eyes enrages me. Is she trying to test me, to see if I'll break? I'll never admit it, but the fact that she claims she'll never have sex with me pisses me off. It only makes me want to prove her wrong, make her beg for it.

"That's fine. I can have any woman I want. I definitely don't have to rape anyone, but since you're so sure you'll never want to have sex with me, I'll remind you of this the next time I have you on your back, your legs spread wide open as I feast on your pink pussy like it's my last meal. All while you beg and plead for me to fuck you, I won't even fucking blink..."

"I was forced into that situation."

"Forced? That's what you call coming on my tongue and screaming my name. Sounds like a really shitty situation."

She blinks slowly, and I notice the rapid rise and fall of her chest as I flick the button on my jeans and shove them down my thighs. My rock hard cock springs free since I'm commando, and Harper shakes her head, looking away before I get the chance to tease her.

"I'm taking a shower, care to join me?"

"I'd rather rot in hell, thank you."

"That can be arranged too." I walk buck ass naked over to the dresser and pull out a pair of boxers and a T-shirt. "Put this on, and I'm sure I don't have to tell you what happens if you disappear while I'm in the shower." I turn to her and find her staring at my backside. Her cheeks flame and she looks away knowing she's been caught.

I would never sleep with you, my ass. The girl is begging to be fucked.

"Of course. Disobey the king's rules, and he'll take everything from me, including my scholarship. How could I ever forget that?"

"Good, I'm glad you remember. I'll be back in a few." I do my best to shower quickly, but having some space between us helps ease the tension in my body. Being around her brings back old feelings, feelings I spent forever burying, trying to forget.

After drying off, I don't bother to wrap a towel around me, and just walk out naked again. I like the shade of pink on her cheeks too much not to. Walking back into my room, my dick is already semi-hard, thinking about who is waiting in my bed.

I step closer and find Harper curled up in the center of the mattress, wearing the clothes I gave her. I don't understand why I stop walking and just stare at her, but I do. She looks so majestic and beautiful like an angel. Her hand is tucked under her cheek, her lips slightly parted, and her breathing slow and even.

Like this, I can really see her beauty, see the girl I fell in love with years ago. Even through the image she portrays to me, I can still see slivers of who she used to be, and I crave that part of her so badly, I'd give anything to have her back.

No. She betrayed you. She didn't want you. The thoughts leave an inky imprint on my brain, and I push them to the back of my mind.

I can't and won't have her...I won't. I'm not that same stupid boy with his heart in his hand. I'm more than that. Crossing the distance to the bed, I crawl into it, still naked. It'll be a nice surprise for her in the morning.

She stirs lightly as I move behind her, tugging her into my chest. Warmth fills my cold chest cavity, my heart thundering so loudly, I can hear it in my ears. Ignoring the stupid flutter of the organ, I tug the blanket from the end of the bed and pull it up and over us.

"Mmmm," she murmurs in her sleep, pushing back against my cock. Mmmm is right. In the morning, we'll continue our little cat and mouse game.

Burying my nose in her hair, I inhale her sweet floral scent, letting the smell sink deep into my lungs, I close my eyes.

"Good night, Harper," I whisper, loving, and hating this moment all at once.

Don't get attached!

8

HARPER

I wake up disoriented, unsure where I am at first. I try and sit up, but I'm tugged backward against a chest. *What the—* I guess last night wasn't a nightmare. Part of me had hoped to wake up this morning and realize yesterday was just my imagination going wild. But apparently, this is my reality. Moving carefully, trying not to wake him, I scoot away. The sheets are softer than I expected them to be beneath my fingers. I don't remember anything happening last night. Warren took a shower, and I changed but fell asleep before he was finished.

So, I'm guessing he just let me be and fell asleep with me. Who knew he could make choices that didn't revolve around being an asshole?

"Where do you think you're going?" Warren's raspy voice fills the room. It has the effect of ice water being poured over my body. Involuntarily, I shiver, and my nipples harden against the thin fabric of my... well, his shirt.

"Getting away from you." I try and roll away, but instead, I end up on my back, with him hovering above me. Something thick and hard presses against my thigh, and my lips part on a gasp. *Morning-wood.* I don't remember it being that hard when it was in my mouth.

"Without helping me relieve this massive hard-on? I think not." His chocolate brown eyes are still filled with sleep, but beneath that, there is a fire burning. The flames grow with each second, threatening to burn me if I get too close. And yet, I want to get close. I want to be burnt. I want to see him melt beneath my touch. I want to see if I have the same effect on him as he does on me.

"I'm not fucking you or giving you a blow job. But I'll beat you off."

Warren blinks, shock overtaking his features, and after a second, he talks, "Wait, you're serious?" He rolls off me, landing on the mattress with a huff.

I cock a brow. "Can't handle being at my mercy?"

His lips curve into a sinister smirk, "Show me your worst, baby. I like it hard and fast, think you can handle it?"

I want to roll my eyes. I've never given a handjob myself, but I have watched enough porn to know how it works. Matter of fact, I'm a little excited to try it out. Shoving up into a sitting position, I let my gaze wander over his perfect body. It's a shame such a horrible monster gets to look this good.

Like a Greek god, his entire body is cut from stone, each muscle, each dip, and plane from his shoulders, down his chest, and over his abs, that lead down to a well-defined v. He's perfect all over, and it's disgusting, because someone as cruel as him, shouldn't get to look like this.

"Like the view?" He winks, and I feel my cheeks heating. Stupid hormones.

"The view is nice. The person attached to it, not so much." I reach for his cock, not even sure why I'm doing this. I shouldn't want to touch him, not after all that he's done to me, but I can't deny myself this one chance to watch him break.

He gives me a bored expression. "Stop talking and get on with the handjob, or I'll find another use for your mouth." I know it's not an idle threat. He's made it before and followed through. As soon as my hand makes contact with the silky skin, he hisses. I squeeze the flesh, reveling in the touch of his smooth length. Then, I start to move, up and down, up and down. His length moves through my hand easily, and after a few strokes, I peer up at him.

His eyes are soft, his normally rough, hardened features are relaxed, and I swear, he looks ten times more handsome in this state.

"Fuck, your hand feels so good."

I chew on my bottom lip, feeling my own arousal start to pool in my core. Warmth fills every pore on my body as I watch the mushroom head disappear and pop back up with each stroke. Warren starts to pant, his perfect chest rising and falling faster and faster.

"Squeeze me, squeeze my cock like your pussy will." I don't bother to correct him, don't bother telling him that my pussy won't do anything for his cock. I'm too caught up in what's going on, the way he melts into the mattress, practically begging me to keep going. Power surges through me, and I squeeze him tighter.

"Fuck me, shit, keep doing that, and I'm going to come..."

"Isn't that the point?" I release my lip and whisper.

A second later, he arches his hips and tips his head back into the pillows.

"Shit, shit. I'm coming..." My heart rate picks up, and my stomach clenches. Heat bubbles over inside of my core, and I want him. I want him to take the ache away. I want my bully, the monster, to ease my pain. One last stroke, and he erupts. Sticky, white cum leaves his tip in quick thick ropes, and I stare at them, becoming mesmerized by them.

My strokes become softer as he calms down from his release. When the last drops of his release bead the tip of his cock, and his whole body shutters, I pull my hand away. At the loss of touch, a coldness sweeps over me.

"I can't believe I thought you were honest when you told me you wanted to wait..." He shakes his head, and in a flash, I'm reminded of all the times he wanted to have sex, and I turned him down.

He wanted me so badly, as badly as I wanted him, but I just wasn't ready. I was insecure and scared, he was confident and didn't have a worry in the world. It wasn't that I didn't want him to be my first, it was just I wasn't ready yet. I was afraid. Of the pain, of what would happen to us afterward.

"Of course, that was all a lie. You were ready, all right. You just didn't want it to be me."

Why does he keep saying these things? Like missing puzzle pieces, his behavior makes no sense to me. Why does he keep assuming that I'm experienced, that I'm some chick that fucks any guy that looks her way?

"I don't understand... I've never..." In a second flat, he goes from being relaxed and calm to the same horrid man he was before. A dark mask covers his face, taking the man I fell in love with when I was a teenager away.

"Shut your fucking mouth." He slams his huge hand over my mouth and shoves me onto the mattress on my back. Like a deer caught in the headlights of a moving car, I peer up at him. He looks like an animal protecting its meal. His eyes are so dark, no light can be seen in them. I whimper underneath his hand but don't dare move.

He looks as if he would snap my neck in a second if I did. Using his other hand, he trails it up my thigh, his nails scraping against my skin. Both pain and pleasure erupt inside me.

"I can't believe I used to want you, used to love you..." he laughs bitterly.

When he makes it to the boxers I'm wearing, he dips a finger into the waistband and pulls them down my legs. This strange feeling consumes me, this is wrong, and I shouldn't want this, but I do. I slightly part my legs, giving him a silent invite.

Without a care in the world, he enters me, his thick fingers sliding into me with ease.

The cruelness in his eyes makes my heart crack right down the middle, "I knew you'd be wet for me. This is your thing. You like it when I take from you."

I shake my head, trying to deny it, but there's no point. He wouldn't believe me anyway, not with the way my body is reacting to him right now. I can feel the pleasure building, his strokes growing faster, each dip inside, bringing me closer to the finale.

"Fuck, I have to taste your lips," he purrs and pulls back his hand. I suck a precious breath of air into my lungs, but he steals it with his kiss in the next moment. There is so much raw anger, pain, and hate in that kiss that for a moment, I think I might drown in the emotions. There is no saving us. Warren and I, we're on a roller coaster, headed down the hill and off the tracks.

With his lips on mine and his fingers working delicious magic on my pussy, I start to lift my hips, meeting his strokes, wanting him deeper, needing more.

"Fuck, yes, come on my hand, cream all over my fingers."

He encourages me with his filthy mouth, whispering against my swollen lips. Like a waterfall gushing water over the cliff's edge, I fall apart, clenching down on his finger while I do. My eyes drift closed, and my body shakes with tremors of pleasure.

My descent back to planet Earth is a slow one, and when I open my eyes, I find Warren staring at me. A look very similar to my own from earlier on his face now. He's studying me like I'm something he can fix.

"You look so beautiful when you come, it's a shame others get to see you like that."

I open my mouth to say something, anything, but Warren pins me with a stare that leaves me completely frozen. It's dark, cruel, and menacing. Above all, it scares me.

"Don't you dare open your mouth to lie to me again. I don't want to fucking hear it. Keep your lips shut. One peep and I'll pull the rug out from underneath you. I'll make you disappear from this place as fast as you reappeared. Do you understand?"

Nodding my head, I watch in complete shock as he gets up and walks away from me. Like I didn't just give him a handjob. Like he didn't just make me come.

After today, I'm more confused than I've ever been.

What does Warren think I did, and how do I fix this? Do I even want to at this point? This is so intense, he is intense.

"Put this on," he throws some sweatpants and a thick sweater at me, followed by a pair of socks. It's a little overkill, but I gladly oblige, dressing in the warm, soft fabric. I watch him pull some shorts and a shirt on, enjoying the view much more than I should.

"Come on, let's get something to eat," he tells me while opening the door. I get up from the bed and follow him through his house like a lost puppy. The place is huge, bigger than any house I've ever lived in, or ever will. Honestly, I've only been inside one house that was bigger than this one, and that's the house Warren grew up in.

When we get closer to what I assume is the kitchen, I start to hear voices. Two guys talking about a football game that's coming up this weekend.

"Are those your roommates," I ask before we enter the room. I know one of them has to be the guy from last night, the one screwing that chick on the couch right out in the open.

"Yes. Don't talk to them. Just be quiet. Be seen, and not heard," he orders me like I'm his servant or something. *Asshole.*

As soon as we walk into the spacious kitchen, that has marble and state of the art appliances, I'm glad Warren gave me clothes to cover every inch of flesh because the moment his roommates, Cameron and Easton, see me, they look at me like I grew a second head. Their stares are so weird, it makes me feel exposed like they can see me even through the thick clothing.

"Stop staring at her," Warren growls and walks to the fridge. He opens it and looks around inside.

"Hey, Harper," Easton greets me, once he recovers from the initial shock of me being here. Before I can reply, Warren pops his head out of the fridge and cuts in.

"Don't fucking talk to her either. Harper, sit down and wait for your food," he talks down to me like I'm a misbehaving child. I'm close to snapping and having a full-blown tantrum.

"Jesus, why are you being such a dick?" Cameron smirks as if knowing what he says is only going to piss his friend off more. Warren's face tenses, his jaw turning to stone. He looks like he might explode from the anger alone or at least punch through the wall.

Being the bigger person and not wanting him to actually start a fistfight with his roommates over looking or talking to me, I do what he says and take a seat at the table. I turn away from the guys and look out of the window, which seems to calm Warren a little.

After a few moments, I sneak a glance over at Warren and notice the tense look in his eyes seems to be dissipating.

He scrambles eggs in a pan, not even paying his roommates a lick of attention.

"We're gonna head out," Cameron announces.

"Finally," Warren mumbles, just as he places the eggs and some toast on a plate.

Easton winks at me as he walks out, and I give him a tiny wave goodbye when Warren isn't looking.

Warren takes the seat next to me, placing a plate and a fork in front of me. I grab it and start eating after I mumble, "Thanks."

We eat in silence until Warren gets up and gets us some orange juice from the fridge, handing it to me, he orders, "Drink."

"Is that how it's going to be now? You tell me what to do, and I do it?"

"Yes, I'm glad you finally get it."

I can't believe that he thinks this is going to work. Does he really think I'm going to let him treat me like this? Then again, what choice do I have? It's this or lose my scholarship and a chance of a good life.

My head feels like it's about to explode. I just need space and time to think, even if it's just for a few hours. I need to be alone, away from him, and I will be. He can't be with me every second of the day. The first chance I get, I'll be gone. I need to go somewhere he won't find me.

9

WARREN

Where the fuck is she? I've looked everywhere, asked everybody I know, and called her phone a million times. Of course, it doesn't matter how many times I call a phone that's turned off, because not a single call is going through.

Pacing through my room, I contemplate my next move. One thing is for sure, I can't stay here, I need to fucking find her. I'm going insane.

There is one place I haven't been to, and I'm dreading finding her there. Easton told me he saw Harper at Night Shift, a local strip club. If I find her there, I don't know what I'm going to do. I don't know if I can hold on to my sanity or my anger.

Bursting out of my room, I walk down the long hallway and end up at Easton's door. I knock twice before he opens it, his black hair is wet, and he's wearing nothing but a towel around his waist.

"Great, you just showered. Now get dressed, we're going to Night Shift."

"I was about to tell you to fuck off, but you had me at Night Shift. I could use some cheap pussy. I'll be ready in five." He closes the door in my face, and like an impatient child, I wait at the front door, checking the time every thirty seconds.

When he finally comes out after four and a half minutes, I huff loudly. The fucker grins at me while walking down the hall as if he is on a morning stroll. Twisting the knob so hard, I fear it might come off, I open the door and step outside.

Easton is right behind me as I get into the car and let the engine roar to life. He is barely inside before I pull out of the driveway.

"Why are you in such a hurry? The girls will be there all night, buddy."

"I'm only going for one girl, and if she is there, well, I'm just telling you now, I'll probably need you to bail me out of jail. That's the only reason I'm taking you."

"Ah, of course... Harper, right?" Even hearing her name out of someone else's mouth enrages me. I know it's completely irrational, but I can't help it. It makes me want to slug Easton in the face more than usual.

"Yes, Harper," I say through clenched teeth while gripping the steering wheel a little tighter. The place is across town, but since I break every speed limit on the way there, it only takes us a few minutes to arrive.

As I park under the pink and yellow neon sign, my blood pressure has reached a new high. I'm torn between wanting her to be here just so I know where she is and praying she'd never step a foot in this place at all.

"Don't worry, I'll make sure you don't go to jail. Come on," Easton climbs out of the car, and I follow closely behind him. When he opens the door, and we head in, my stomach churns, and I feel like I'm going to vomit.

I've been here a few times and always enjoyed it before. It's easier when the girls are just random bodies and not the girl who stole your heart in high school. Easton pays our cover charge, and the sleazeball at the front pushes away the curtain for us.

Walking in on unsteady feet, I scan the dimly lit room like a fucking hawk. My eyes skim over every girl I see, long legs, big tits, round ass. Each girl looks like the next. Then I pause... dark brown wavy hair meets my eyes. Her back is turned to me, but her curves are all too familiar. Red hot rage pulses through my veins. I force my legs to work, to take me over to where she is standing at the bar, chatting up some potential *customers*. Bile rises in my throat when I think about what she is doing here, who has seen her... touched her.

Motherfucker, I have to stop before I commit murder.

She raises her slender hand, her finger grazes some guy's arm, and I snap like a rubber band. Closing the distance between us in two large strides, I grab her by the shoulder and pull her away from the guy and into my chest.

Mine. She's mine.

Harper screams into my chest, while two huge bouncers come running toward us. I'm vaguely aware of Easton yelling something behind me, but I'm too far gone to make out the words. Harper twists in my hold, placing her hands on my chest, trying to push me away. Her eyes find mine, and that's the moment I realize that I've fucked up.

"What the fuck, Warren?" She yells at me, although it's not who I thought *she* was.

"Valerie?" Her name barely leaves my mouth when one of the bouncers shoves me back and away from her. "I thought... you were..."

"You know this punk?" One of the beefed-up guys eyeballs me while rolling his shoulders.

"Yes," Valerie, waves the guys away. "He is fine, don't worry. He just wants a lap dance. Isn't that, right?"

I roll my eyes, "Yeah, a lap dance."

Valerie grabs my arm and pulls me to the back of the place where they have a hand full of small private rooms.

"You better pay me double for this," Valerie huffs when we are alone in one of the rooms. She pushes a button on the wall, and some low, sexy song starts playing. "You really didn't think Harper was here, did you?"

"Someone told me they saw her here," I explain, just now realizing that who Easton probably saw was Valerie. They do look very similar. Same hair color, same curvy frame. Which isn't that surprising, seeing as they're cousins.

Valerie shakes her head, "Warren, it's like you don't know the girl at all. She would never work in a strip club. God, the girl is such a prude. I'm pretty sure she is still a virgin."

Ha, she's funny. "Well, I can guarantee you that she is not. Do you know where she's at? I haven't seen her, and her phone is shut off."

"Really? That's unlike her." Valerie taps her chin, "Honestly, I have no idea where she could be. I've been kind of a bitch to her lately. She isn't too fond of me right now, and I haven't talked to her." She shrugs, and I remember how she talked down to Harper at the party, and I have to agree, she's been a bitch.

"Call me if you hear from her, okay?" I take out my wallet and fish out two one-hundred-dollar bills. Valerie takes the money without batting an eye, stuffing the bills in her tiny silver triangle bikini top.

"I will, but if you talk to her first, please don't tell her I work here. I'll never hear the end of it. I told her I work at a diner, and I don't want to be lectured like a child."

I couldn't care less about what Valerie wants or thinks. All that matters to me right now is finding Harper.

"You really can't think of a place she would go? Friends she might want to go see?" I'm half-tempted to ask her about any guys she might be seeing but bite my tongue.

"Warren…" Valerie looks at me like I'm stupid. Placing her hand on her hip, she starts to explain, "Are you blind or something? Harper doesn't have any friends. She is too worried about her grades. I had to drag her to that last party, and I'd bet all the cash I have on me tonight that she won't be going to anymore, at least not with me."

For the first time since Harper returned in my life, doubt about how I've perceived her creeps up on me. I thought she worked here. I was sure she had been dating tons and partied with friends. But really, looking at it now, analyzing the last few days, I guess I was wrong. It's starting to seem like I did all the partying and fucking while Harper hit the textbooks.

That thought has me asking my next question, "Did Harper date after we broke up?"

"Not that I know of," she tells me, and I believe her. I don't think she would lie for Harper, not after the way she treated her. Valerie just cares about herself.

The thing is, even though I'm relieved Harper hasn't had a boyfriend, she still cheated on me back then. She still gave her virginity to someone else, and that's completely unforgivable. I told her I would wait for her, but waiting wasn't what she wanted.

Valerie shifts her weight impatiently back and forth on her feet. "The song is over, either you pay me again, or you get out."

"I'll leave. So you can get back to your other customers," I say, reaching for the door handle.

"Not everyone is born with a golden spoon in their mouth. Don't look down at people who work for their money. For some of us, this is how we make ends meet." The thought brings forth a memory that crashes into me like a wave, taking me out at the knees.

A little girl with thick hair, the color of cinnamon and chocolate, comes running through the foyer, a big toothy grin on her face. Daddy doesn't like it when we run, or play, or smile. I'm pretty sure he hates anything that doesn't involve being in his office.

He usually tells me that I should only talk when I'm spoken to. Be seen, not heard.

"Harper Mae," the maid scolds as the girl I now know as Harper almost crashes into me. Harper's smile falls and turns into a frown a second later, as the maid grabs her by the wrist and tugs her into her side. She's so pretty, like an angel, and strangely, I want to see her smile again. Clasping my hands together in front of me, I stare at her in awe.

"I'm so sorry, Warren," Maid Claudia apologizes, her face stricken with worry. I'm sure most of the maids have families and kids, but this is the first time I've ever seen another kid my age running around the house.

"It's okay." I smile and stare at her for a little longer. I dig deep, building up the courage to ask her if she wants to play with my power rangers with me. This huge house makes me feel alone, so having a friend would be nice.

"Do you... do you want to..." The words don't even make it past my lips when my father walks into the room. I look up at him, taking note of the sour look on his face.

"Run along, Warren, you need to find some other children to play with. Children of your own status."

My brow furrows in confusion. I'm not sure what that means. My own status? What does that mean? We're both kids, and I bet she likes power rangers too, who doesn't?

"I'm sorry, Mr. Williams. I didn't have a babysitter. I had to bring her, but she won't bother anyone, I promise. Isn't that right, Harper?"

"Yes," Harper whispers, holding on to her mother's leg.

"I don't care if you bring her as long as she doesn't touch anything. If she breaks something, it's coming out of your paycheck." Then he turns his attention back to me. "Warren, run along," my father says in a stern voice. Even though I don't want to, I walk away, knowing if I disobey Daddy, nothing good will come from it.

Like a slingshot, my brain propels me back to the present. That was my very first memory of Harper.

I don't say anything because there isn't anything else to say. Walking back out to the stage, I find Easton making sex eyes at one of the girls on stage.

"Let's go, douchebag," I yell over the music. Of course, he's too mesmerized by the chick's tits to pay me any attention. Using my last shred of patience, I walk over to him and slap him upside the head. "I'm leaving, fuckhead."

"Dude, what the fuck?" he growls, but I'm already walking away. I'm not going to stay in this strip club and babysit him all night long. Not when I have no fucking idea where Harper is. Thousands of thoughts assault me at once. Someone already broke into her apartment. What if something happened? My stomach twists. Or maybe she's doing this on purpose to hurt me, to push me over the edge because of the way I acted this morning.

When I reach the car, I find that Easton did follow me. Smart thinking. Climbing into the car, I sit in the driver's seat, trying to figure out where the hell to go next. My fingers drum against the steering wheel without thought.

"What are we going to do now? You look as lost as you did when you came in here? I'm guessing Valerie wasn't of any help?"

"Well, I mean she was, and she wasn't. She doesn't know where Harper is, but she did shed some light on a couple of things. I think I may have been wrong about her."

"What do you mean by that?" Confusion bleeds into Easton's face.

I shake my head. I don't have time to explain this to him.

"Let's just say I was wrong." At least about what she's been up to the last few years. I start the car and pull out of the parking spot.

"Where are we going?" he asks a second later.

"To find Harper," I answer without ever taking my eyes off the road.

10

HARPER

"You can come home whenever you want, sweetie," my mother assures me as if I need to be told twice. I love spending time with my parents. I'd take a home-cooked meal over cafeteria slop any day, but both of them work so hard running their cleaning business, the last thing I want is to be a burden to them.

That's why I worked so hard for my scholarship, and why I live off-campus, so I can save up every little bit of money I have to buy the things I need over asking my parents for money.

"I know, Mom," I give her a smile. "I've just been busy. Classes are crazy, and the workload is a lot. You know how I get about my grades." That's not a lie. At least not fully. Though the only thing crazy at Blackthorn is Warren.

"Yes, yes," her hazel eyes soften, and she reaches into her pocket, "your father and I want you to have this. You never ask for anything, and we know you have the scholarship, but maybe you could use the cash for something."

I open my mouth to object, but my mother shakes her head and grabs my hand, pressing the warm dollar bills into it.

"Take it, please." The pleading in her voice stops me in my tracks. Even though I don't want to take it, I bite the inside of my cheek and take it, nodding my head.

She smiles and releases my hand. I shove the wad of cash into my pocket, bumping into my phone. *Shit.* My phone. It's been off all day. I can't imagine the shit storm I'll be walking back into when I get back to Blackthorn.

I know without a doubt that Warren is pissed, probably ripping the campus to shreds trying to find me. Something that feels like satisfaction coats me from the inside out. For once, I outsmarted him, tricked him. I left without him even knowing.

Pulling out my phone, I turn the device on. As soon as the thing is on, it starts to go off, just as I suspected it would.

"Popular, huh?" My mom grins, her eyes lighting up as she makes another loaf of bread. If she isn't cleaning for a living, she's cooking. It's like she doesn't know what relaxation is.

"Yeah," I lie, refusing to tell her it's some crazed asshole who thinks he can control me and everything I do. Looking down at my phone, I find I have thirty text messages or more, plus numerous voicemails.

It's a good thing I'm heading back to Blackthorn today. God forbid the psycho go an entire night without me. Walking into the tiny living room, I prepare myself to calm him and almost chuckle when my phone starts ringing, his name flashing across the screen.

I hit the green answer key and hold the phone to my ear.

"Yes, can I help you?" I speak calmly into the receiver. I shouldn't want to stir the pot of crazy, but I do. Warren deserves to feel the same pain I have.

"What the fuck, Harper? Where are you? I've looked everywhere for you. I swear to god, you better have a good excuse. You didn't think you could escape me..."

"I'm not stupid, Warren. I just needed some time away from you. You're mental, and it's exhausting dealing with you."

"Where are you?" Is all he says, his voice clipped.

"On my way back to Blackthorn. I'll be leaving in a few minutes to catch the bus."

"No, you won't. Stay right where you fucking are. I'll come and pick you up." An objection sits heavy on my tongue, but Warren interrupts me before I can speak. "And if you think about disobeying me, I'll march right up to the administration building and tell them everything I know."

"Your threats are getting old," I taunt.

"And you're going to regret doing this. Send me the address, now. I'll be there asap, and if you were with another guy... Harper, I will go to prison. Right after I kill him."

I roll my eyes, "You don't own me, and we aren't even together, but if it's going to stop you from committing murder, I can assure you I wasn't with a guy. I'm at my parents' house."

There's a brief pause, and I wonder what he's thinking, "Text me the address, and stay put." He orders like I'm a dog before he hangs up the phone. For a second, I consider not texting him, turning my phone back off, and staying here, but decide against it.

Minus Warren, I love Blackthorn. The teachers are kind, and the work is easy. Attending such a high-profile college is going to get me the best job once I graduate, so I can't mess this up. This education is going to last me a lifetime, Warren is only going to last the time it takes me to get this degree.

Gritting my teeth, I type out the address and hit send. It was nice to have a little peace, but I guess it's time to get back to being terrorized.

AN HOUR LATER, Warren pulls up to my parents' tiny house in a blacked-out SUV. I kiss my mother on the cheek, grab my bag and walk outside. No point in elongating the inevitable. If I don't go out there, then he'll come in here, and that's the last thing I want.

I make it out the door and three steps onto the sidewalk before he's at my side. The first thing I notice is his eyes. They're so dark they might as well be black. The second thing I notice is that he looks tired, really tired.

Guilt niggles at me, but I push it away. Why should I feel guilty about leaving to visit my parents? Why should I feel guilty when he is crazy, and I'm nothing but a possession to him?

"That was a pretty reckless stunt. I thought you were smarter than that." His fingers wrap around my wrist, and he pulls me to the SUV, basically dragging me along the way.

"You're right, it would have been smarter not to tell you where I was."

"You think so? You think I would've stopped looking for you?" He growls into my ear, and I can feel the heat of his breath on my skin. I shiver, my body responding to his closeness.

Why do I want him? Even when he's mean and cruel—so cruel it hurts—a small part of me still clings to him, craves his presence.

"Never. The answer is never. You're mine, every fucking inch of you is mine. When you chose to stay instead of walking away, you gave yourself to me."

The possessiveness in his voice is something I've never heard or even felt before. Opening the door for me, he shoves me into the passenger seat, then slams the door shut. Shifting in the seat, I'm stunned into silence because I'm not sure how this will end. Where is this going? I still haven't figured out why he thinks all these horrible things about me, and I'm not sure how to get it out of him either.

When he gets in and starts driving, the tension in the vehicle mounts. It's so heavy I can barely breathe. Warren white knuckles the steering wheel, probably envisioning it as my neck.

"I need to ask you something... and you need to tell me the truth. This is really important." His voice is a little calmer than before, and there is a weird urgent need to his tone as well.

"Okay, what is it?"

"When we were dating... or before, did someone hurt you?" His question catches me completely off guard. I don't know what I expected, but it wasn't this.

"What do you mean, hurt me?"

"Like abused you, raped you, or hurt you in any other way?"

"What? No! Why would you ask me that?" I'm so confused by his question. Where is this coming from?

"Are you sure?" He presses.

"Yes, Warren. No one hurt me. Not when we were dating, not before or after. I swear."

Just when I thought I couldn't get any more confused, he gets angry again. Hitting the side of the steering wheel like that's the only way he can channel his uncontainable fury.

"I'm going to have so much fun fucking you, making you scream my name. I'll make you regret everything. Make you beg for my forgiveness."

"I didn't do anything... all I did was go and see my parents.

I've never hurt you." Out of the corner of my eye, I see his body vibrating.

Is he going to hurt me? Punish me? Explode into the hulk? I don't understand why he's acting this way, why he blows up like this.

"Stop! Stop talking. I don't want to hurt you, Harper. I really don't, not physically, at least, but I'm close to losing my fucking shit, and I don't know what will happen when I do."

His confession has me pressing my lips into a tight line. With my chin to my chest, I stare at the floor. Closing my eyes to get away from him, I somehow manage to drift off to sleep.

A short while later, I come to. Warren is carrying me. Lifting my head off his chest, I notice that we're at his house.

"I want to go home," I mumble tiredly. All of this back and forth with him is exhausting. I just want to go to my place right now.

"Yeah, that's never going to happen. You belong to me now. I don't know why you can't get this into your head. When I tell you to jump, you'll ask how high? When I tell you to spread your legs, you'll ask how wide? When you go to class, I'll be there waiting for you. You. Are. Mine." He speaks each word with a deepness and darkness that makes me believe him.

As soon as we enter his room, he tosses me onto the bed like a doll, and I scurry backward and away from him. All my sleepiness is suddenly gone, leaving me wide awake and on high alert. He shuts the door, the sound much too soft for the raging storm that I know is brewing inside of him.

When he turns to face me again, it's like every shred of who he is, who I've known him to be, is gone. Even in his darkest moments, I could still see the human beneath the mask, but right now, I can't see any humanity.

"It's funny, you were so tough-sounding over the phone.

Where is that girl now? With her strong backbone and spitfire tongue?" He's taunting me, trying to get me to fight back, but fighting back is what he wants, and I'll be damned if I'm going to give my bully the bullets he needs to shoot me in the heart.

"Warren, please? It doesn't have to be this way."

He tilts his head to the side and even as devilish as he is, he still manages to look gorgeous, "It does have to be like this, and it always will be, because of you. You made us this way."

Watching him stalk over to the bed, I tell myself I can't do this. I'll fight back. I know what's coming. He's going to take from me, take the last thing I have to offer him. It was always meant to be his but never like this.

Grabbing onto my ankle, he tugs me to the edge of the mattress. Tears fill my eyes, and I contemplate my next move. Blanketing his body with mine, he leans into my face. His eyes searching mine, and I shiver at the darkness inside of his. What happened to the boy I loved? Who hurt him? Who destroyed what we had?

Licking his lips, he whispers, "Cry for me, Harper, let me see your tears. I want to taste them, see if your fear tastes as sweet as it looks."

I shake my head, "What happened to make you hate me so much?" I croak, choking on the emotions in my throat. "Just tell me."

In an instant, Warren has his hand wrapped around my throat. The tears I was trying to keep at bay spring from my eyes and trail down my cheeks, leaving cold rivulets behind. He gives my throat a squeeze, and the air in my chest feels like a ton of bricks.

Darting his pink tongue out, he licks the salty tears from my eyes. It's fucked up, so fucked up, but it's also intimate. I don't understand how to explain it.

"I'm going to fuck every ounce of hate I have into you." He licks down to my cheek, stopping at my ear, he nips at the tender lobe. "I'm going to make you feel all the pain you've made me feel. I'm going to destroy all the good inside of you, just like you've destroyed all the good inside me."

Fear pulses through my veins at his words, but to my utter shame, there is a need as well, a need for him to touch me, make me feel what he feels. Maybe that's the only way I'll be able to understand. If he won't tell me what I've done to hurt him, maybe he'll show me. It's a risky move... and I shouldn't even consider giving myself over to him, but if this is the only way, then I'll do it.

11

WARREN

I'm doing everything I can to keep myself in line. I want to hurt Harper, mark her body, but something is stopping me. There is a softness in her eyes that I don't understand. She looks afraid, but she also looks like she's willing to give herself over to me, as if she knows deep down that's what she needs.

Stupid girl. Stupid for running away from me. Stupid for thinking she could escape. Stupid. Stupid. Stupid. I squeeze her throat a little harder, and she whimpers like a scared animal.

With my other hand, I sneak under her shirt. My fingers move all on their own, gently grazing over her smooth skin. She feels like silk in my hands, slowly slipping away from me, but I can't let her go, *won't* let her go. Reaching the edge of her bra, I trace my finger against it, watching as her eyes grow wide, and her chest swells.

Grazing her hardened nipple through the thin fabric, I watch with fascination as she bites her bottom lip, trying to stop herself from reacting to my touch. Little does she know, by the time I'm done with her, she won't be able to do anything but scream my name.

Rolling the bud between two fingers, I release her throat so I can use my hand to pop the button on her jeans. Even as afraid as she might be, I know she wants this. She can't hide her arousal. I bet the moment I touch her pretty pussy, she'll melt into me, spread her legs, and plead with me to take her.

Staring into her eyes, I slip beneath the waistband of her panties and trail down over her mound. My fingers move lower, and I graze her folds, dipping the edge of my pointer finger into her sweet honey. Of course. I knew she'd be wet, so it's no surprise when I feel her arousal on my fingertip.

"You might be afraid, but your body knows how good I'll make this for you." I move my hand lower until I'm cupping her entire pussy in my hand. All-fucking-mine. "Tell me you want this. Tell me you want to be fucked by the monster that I am, and I'll do it. I'll fuck you so hard the entire house will hear us."

Hesitation flickers in her eyes, she's still searching for the boy I used to be, the guy she used to know, the one who would've given her the entire fucking world if she had asked for it. But he's gone, broken, burned by her betrayal.

"If you're looking for any part of the old me, you won't find him. This is who I am now, who I will always be. So, tell me, do you want this? Do you want me to fuck you?"

She chokes on a sob, and I pull my hand away, giving her nipple a hard pinch.

"Yes..." She says breathlessly.

"Strip out of your clothes and then get back on the bed." On shaking legs, she moves off the bed. I strip out of my own clothing in the time it takes her to take off her pants. She's stalling, and my patience is growing thin.

I don't even know why I care to fuck her, maybe to give myself a taste, to tell myself she wasn't really worth it. I could have any chick I want, and yet, no one gets my pulse-pounding like she does. My hate for her is becoming an obsession, but it doesn't matter. She's mine. Always has been and always will be, the only difference, now I'll make sure she remembers it. I won't ever let someone else touch her again.

Slowly, she peels her shirt off and undoes her bra. Both items fall to the floor, landing softly. I take in her naked body before me. If perfection could be described and put into a person, she would be it. But it's an illusion... she's not perfect. She's evil, a wolf in sheep's clothing, and this time I won't let her fool me. This time, I'm ready...I see her, really see her.

Taking a step forward, I press both hands to her full perky breasts. She lets out a shudder at my touch, and I grin. Giving her a gentle shove against the chest, she takes the hint and steps backward and away from my touch.

"Get on the bed," I order.

"Warren," she pleads, crawling up onto the mattress.

"It's time to pay up, sweetheart." I fist my cock in my hand and stalk over to the bed. So pretty, and so completely fucked. Spreading her legs with my hand, I drop my gaze down to her pretty pink pussy. "Do you have any diseases I have to be worried about?"

"Of course, not."

"Are you on birth control?"

"Yes..." She opens her mouth to continue, but I press a finger against her soft lips.

"That's all I needed to know," I whisper, tugging her ass to the edge of the bed. Moving my hand away from her lips, I trail it down her chest, between her breasts and over her smooth stomach. I try not to get lost in the way she looks beneath me, but it's always been a dream of mine. In my mind, I always thought I would be her first, but she took that from me... the thought hits me right in the chest like a bullet being shot from a gun, it shatters every thought I have about her.

"I always thought..." I start but stop. No point in telling her something that she never cared about to start with. Spreading both thighs, I take my cock and rub it against her folds, gathering the juices that are there. It's time for revenge, it's time for me to fuck her memory from my mind. Her juices glisten against my blunt head, and I bring it back to her entrance pressing against the hole.

She lets out a small whimper as I drive my hips forward, seeking the confines of her tight and warm pussy. Pure bliss encompasses me. I've fucked a lot of women, but none have ever felt like this. Like... home.

Harper struggles beneath me, her entire body shaking. Leaning forward, I cage her face with my arms so I can stare into her eyes. Tears slip down her cheeks, and all I can do is stare at them. There is something there, in her eyes, but I can't bring myself to reach out and grab it. I'm too far gone to care, too high on anger, and revenge.

Pulling out, I slam back into her, hissing at the pleasure that ripples through me.

I knew it would be good, real good, but I didn't expect it to feel like heaven.

"Fuck," I growl, burying my face in her neck. She smells like vanilla and flowers, a smell that's intoxicating. Harper sinks her nails into my skin, marking me, and I welcome the pain as I thrust in and out of her at a feverish pace. Soft whimpers fill the room as I rut into her, claiming her over and over again just like I should've three years ago before she gave herself to some other bastard.

The pleasure at the base of my spine builds with every deep thrust inside her tight channel, and I know I should be selfish, come without caring about if she gets pleasure from this or not, but I can't. I want to feel Harper come on my cock too badly. I want her to feel what she has been missing, what she could have had a long time ago.

Balancing my weight on one arm, I snake a hand between us and find her clit. It's hard, and as soon as I start rubbing small circles against it, Harper's whimpers turn into soft moans.

"I shouldn't let you come, you don't deserve it," I whisper against her skin as I press a gentle kiss to her collarbone. "But I won't deny you, because as selfish as I am, I still want you to feel the same way I'm feeling right now."

Fucking her harder and faster, I move my finger against her clit at the same pace until we're both panting and on the verge of unyielding satisfaction.

"You feel too good... I'm going to come..." I grunt, slamming into her. Pulling away so I can see her face, I notice that she too is close. Her eyes are pinched together, and her lips are parted. I grit my teeth and rub her faster, watching with amazement as her eyes flutter open and her mouth forms into a full O. All at once, she bears down on me, squeezing me so tightly, stars appear before my eyes.

At the cusp of her orgasm, mine barrels into me, dragging me down. Forcing me to still, I fill her tightness with every drop of cum inside of my balls until I feel nothing but emptiness.

Sagging against her chest with relief when it's all over, my heart beats furiously. I swallow thickly, trying to figure out what my next move is going to be.

The need to hold her and cuddle up with her in my bed is almost too much. But I can't get attached to her, can't want her any more than I do.

She broke me once, ruined our precious future. This is entirely her fault, and I need to remember that before the guilt sets in.

Pushing off of her, I notice that she winces as I pull out. Maybe she hasn't been with a guy as big as me? I don't know. I don't really care.

"You're free to leave now until I need your pussy again." I shoo her away.

She blinks. Confusion, then burning anger filling her eyes. "If this is how you are going to act, then there won't be a next time." In a flash, she's off the bed, tugging all her clothes back on.

"We'll see about that," I grin, lying back on the mattress, I interlace my fingers and tuck them behind my head.

Her pretty eyes glisten with tears, and seeing her so distraught, so hurt, tugs at me.

"I hate you, Warren. I really, really do. I thought if I did this, I could understand you better, but as it turns out, there isn't anything worth understanding. There isn't a bone in your body that still cares about me..."

And just like that, she walks out, slamming the door shut behind her. It takes every shred of willpower I have to remain on the bed and not chase after her.

Remember, she did this to us. She chose someone else. She lied. She betrayed you. Like a sponge, I soak up every word, repeating them to myself over and over again until the need to go to her disappears.

The image of the bill from the abortion clinic is ingrained in my mind. It's a never-ending nightmare, one that my heart refuses to let me forget. I can still feel the paper in my hand.

I'm staring at the medical bill, confused and angry. Harper's name is written on the top of the paper, and right there in the center is the word abortion. I've read the thing three times, but the words still don't quite make sense.

"I wanted you to know, son," my father's voice fills my ears, but I can't hear him. All I can see is the betrayal right in front of me. I want to ask him why he would show me this, but I already know why. He's hated Harper since the moment I showed interest in her, and this is just another thing to drive his point home.

I've defended her for years, to the ends of the Earth, but I can't justify this.

She wanted to wait...

She wanted to wait...

All so she could go fuck someone else, and get pregnant with his bastard baby? Bitter rage fills my veins. I want to go to her, shake her to death, but instead, I crumple the paper in my hands, my fists clenching with rage.

I need her gone, need her to leave before I do something drastic. I can't believe I trusted her, believed her. That I fucking waited for her.

"I'm sorry, Warren," my father interrupts my thoughts.

"It's fine. I expected this... And since I'm here, I wanted to tell you that I saw her mother stealing food from the pantry." It isn't a lie. I had seen her taking food from the pantry, but never cared to tell my father about it. Everyone needed to eat. That was before though. Before she took my heart and shattered it. Before she made me believe in her love. Before she betrayed me.

Father shakes his head, "Of course, she would be stealing. I'll take care of this. I'll get rid of her and her whoring daughter."

The memory fades, but the pain remains.

Her betrayal is something I doubt I'll ever forget. It feels like I've lost a loved one, and in a way, I guess I did. The girl I loved became nothing...in the blink of an eye.

12

HARPER

*L*ast night, I went home and straight to bed. If I had my way, I would still be curled up in that bed right now, but I can't miss my classes, which is why I'm dragging myself to the coffee shop for some much-needed caffeine before heading to chemistry.

I slept terribly and not just because of what happened yesterday. It was the thought of someone breaking into my place again, that had me worried to close my eyes.

I keep telling myself that it was just some druggy looking for dope or money and that it won't happen again, but that, of course, is a steaming load of crap. Anyone can break in again at any time. The doors on these apartments are a joke. I'm pretty sure I could kick them in. And if someone comes into my place, I'm completely screwed since my self-defense skills are non-existent.

When Warren first told me to stay at his house, I thought it was stupid, but now I wish I was still there with him... *safe*.

Ha, safe. I'm not safe with him or at my house, but being with him at night is the lesser of two evils. I might sorta hate

Warren, but I know he wouldn't hurt me like someone else might.

A familiar feeling washes over me at the thought of him, and right away, I know what it is. *Dread.* It's the same one I felt when Warren left me kneeling in that bathroom. All over again, I've become the used and discarded girl I told myself I wouldn't become again.

How could I be so stupid? Giving my virginity to him was supposed to be a good thing, but all it's done is make me feel crummy.

Placing my order with the barista, I walk to the waiting area. My phone starts to ring, and I don't want to look at it. I swear to god if it's Warren, I'm going to toss the thing in the nearest trash can. When I see Valerie's name flash across the screen instead, I'm relieved, but still, I second guess answering it. Every time I talk to her, she treats me like shit. I don't need that right now. I really, really don't.

She's family, and regardless of how I'm feeling, blood is blood. Pressing the green answer key, I bring the phone to my ear, "What's up?"

"Oh, my god, you're alive. I thought you were dead. I tried calling you the other day, and it went to voicemail."

Yeah, 'cause I was trying to escape. "Yeah, sorry, I couldn't find my charger."

"Oh, well, how are you? Are you okay? Did Warren say anything to you?"

"Huh? What do you mean? I talked to Warren yesterday. What was he supposed to say?"

"I... I don't know. I saw him the other day at the gas station. I thought you guys were friends." She stumbles over her words, nervously. Maybe she's on something? It wouldn't be the first time.

"No, no, we aren't friends, and I'm doing fine, thanks for asking."

"I'm sorry about the party... how I acted. I don't know why I get like that sometimes."

Because you're selfish, and you care about being friends with rich kids more than being mine.

"It's fine. Look, I gotta go. I have to get to classes, but I'll talk to you later, okay?"

"Okay, talk later," she tells me and hangs up. The barista calls my name, and I step up to get my drink. I grab the iced latte and give the barista a smile. Walking out of the little coffee shop, I suck the sugary goodness from the straw.

The first taste leaves me feeling a little better than I was a second ago, and I smile. I start walking to my next class, a little more pep in my step than before.

Heading down Kingdom Hall, I open one of the double doors, about to walk through it when I all but stop dead in my tracks. My heart slams into my throat, the air in my lungs ceasing to exist, and I damn near drop my iced latte in the process.

Warren. I hate him. I hate him so much, but I also want him. Want him in ways that I shouldn't because he's a horrible, cruel monster. Forcing myself to make my legs work, I keep walking, taking quick steps. As much as I tell myself not to look, it's not that easy, and even harder when I spot the incredible looking woman hanging off his arm. She could be a model.

She looks nothing like me, and maybe that's the point. I tell myself it's nothing but a game, but that stupid jealously bug rears its ugly head anyway, and I'm left wanting to bite the chick's head off velociraptor style.

Getting closer, I notice another couple is standing with

him, I was too consumed with Warren's presence before, but now I see that it's Parker and his girlfriend, Willow. I've never actually talked to either, but I've heard Warren talking about them.

Willow stares at me, I can feel her eyes burning into my skin as I walk past them. When our eyes clash, she smiles at me. I don't know how to feel about that, so I skew my facial features. Parker has his arm wrapped around her and gives me a brooding look before leaning in and whispering something into Warren's ear.

I don't stick around to see what happens next, and instead, haul ass into the chemistry room. As soon as I enter the room, I find the nearest seat and sink down into it. My lungs burn, and it feels like I wasn't breathing the entire time I walked down that hall.

You're nothing to him. Nothing... I don't know why, but I had stupidly hoped that the way I left his house that day might've knocked some sense into him. After a few minutes, I calm down enough to get my books out. My thoughts are still racing, right along with my heart, but at least I can breathe again.

It's funny how even after everything he's done to me, this jealousy hurts more than anything else. I'd rather have him threaten me, use my body, and humiliate me than go through seeing him with someone else.

The class drags on forever, or at least it feels that way. When it's finally over, I don't think anything we've talked about has stuck in my brain. As I'm packing up my stuff, the professor announces that we have a test next week, and since I couldn't comprehend a single thing today, I know I have a lot of studying to do if I want to ace it.

Since I don't feel like going home to be all alone, going to the library seems like a win-win. The walk to the library takes all of five minutes, and I'm thankful that I don't run into Warren and his flavor of the day on my way.

That would be my luck.

The librarian greets me with a wide smile as I pass the circular desk. I try to give her a similar greeting, but the corners of my mouth just don't want to curl up. I think I'm stuck with a permanent frown now.

Finding some extra reading material, I browse through the shelves, trying to forget anybody that starts with the letter *W*. When I find three books, I sit down at one of the tables, all the way in the corner. The area is secluded, and it makes me feel like I'm in my own little reading fort.

This is another plus of attending this school. The library is pristine in every way. The chair I'm sitting in right now is so comfortable, I bet it cost more than the entire contents of my apartment. No, I don't think, I know.

Opening the first book, I take a deep calming breath. The smell of the paper actually helps my nerves. Running my fingers along the pages, I calm further. I spend the next few hours with my nose between those pages. Studying enough for the next three tests.

By the time I'm done, the library is closing up, and it's already getting dark outside. I quietly curse under my breath, I shouldn't have stayed this long. Walking through my neighborhood after dark is not the best idea, the break-in is a stark reminder of that. But what choice do I have now? Call Warren and ask him to take me in? Ha... not in a million years. I'd rather get mugged.

I check out the books and stuff them all into my backpack. Slinging the heavy bag over my shoulder, I walk outside. Cold wind penetrates my clothes, making me shiver deeply as I start walking toward my place. I'm not even off the campus when I get this eerie feeling that someone is watching me. Turning, I look over my shoulder a few times but don't see anyone.

Making my feet move even faster, my slow walk becomes a slow jog, but I don't make it far before a large figure steps in front of me, cutting me off. It takes a second for my eyes to adjust, but when they do, all I can do is shake my head.

James. The creep from the party.

"Well, hello there," he greets, the tone of his voice is like nails on a chalkboard to my ears. If he's trying to be seductive, it's not working.

"Hi," I say, only trying to be polite and attempt to move past him. He steps sideways to block my way, shaking his head at me.

"Not so fast." He puts his arm out.

"What do you want?" I grip onto my backpack strap a little harder. As it turns out, it's not just the people in my neighborhood I have to worry about. It's here too.

"I heard what you've been telling people about me. That was a mistake, bitch," he growls, taking a step toward me. "Maybe I should show you how big my dick is? Maybe take some pictures while I fill your mouth with it?"

I know a bad situation when I see one, so before he's even done talking, I spin around and start running. I only make it about three steps before he slams into my back, knocking me to the ground. My kneecaps hit the ground so hard, I'm pretty sure I've shattered the bone. Pain shoots through my body like lightning, making me cry out.

On my hands and knees, I try to crawl away from him in a last effort to get away. But his meaty fingers are digging into my arms, pulling me backward. This is a nightmare, a complete nightmare.

Looking around, I hope that someone might see us, anyone, but I wouldn't get that lucky. No one is going to save me. James is going to hurt me, and no one will even know.

"Hey, where do you think you're going? I'm not done with you, not by a long shot." He pulls me back to my feet and starts dragging me behind him. "I'm going to show you what I would have done to you if you were in your apartment than night I came to visit."

My mind is too busy, too panic stricken to make sense of what he is saying right now. All I can think of is fighting him. I don't know where he's taking me. I'm frantically trying to get away from him. Screaming and trying to pull away, doing anything I can to succeed in getting away.

My thoughts get hazy. Then, as if he knows I'm going to draw attention to us eventually, he starts yelling at me to shut up and slaps a hand over my mouth. I do everything I can, bite him, scratch him, and kick him, but he is too strong. He easily overpowers me and continues to drag me to wherever the hell it is he wants to go.

With his arms wrapped so tightly around me, it's hard to breathe, and black spots appear in my vision. *No.* I gasp. For a moment, I think I'm going to pass out, my limbs grow heavy, and my vision blurs.

Then it happens. One second, I'm in James' clutches, about to get raped or worse, and the next, his arms disappear, and my whole body sags to the ground. I fall, landing with a hard thud, but at least I'm not going anywhere with him anymore. My lungs expand, and I suck air in like I haven't been able to breathe for years.

Gentle hands move over my arms and end up engulfing my shaking hands.

"Are you okay?" A girl's voice reaches my ears. With my

vision still blurred, I glance at her face. It's hard to make out her features, but I find kind eyes looking at me with nothing but concern. It only takes me a moment to realize that I've seen her before. She's the girl who was standing with Parker earlier.

"I- I think I'm okay," I say. Even my voice is shaky, and I hate it. I hate being scared and weak and I hate that she's seen me like this.

"You'll be okay. He won't hurt you anymore." She assures me.

Only then do I hear grunts and fists meeting skin in the background. Turning my head against the grass, I see Parker and...Warren, hovering over James. Warren hits him over and over again, and I wonder if Parker is going to stop him.

"He is out, dude, come on," Parker puts his hand on Warren's shoulder, but he just shrugs him off and continues beating James' face relentlessly.

"Warren, stop," Willow calls out for him. "Harper needs to see a doctor."

That gets him to finally stop. Shoving off the grass, he gets up, leaving James' lifeless body on the ground.

Oh, god, did he... kill him? Just as the question enters my mind, James groans and moves around on the floor, but he seems too out of it to get up. Good.

"What's wrong with her?" Warren asks bitterly, and walks over to us, his eyes scanning my body from head to toe.

"Her knees and hands look really bad," Willow explains, making me look down at myself. My jeans are ripped, and my knees are bleeding, and so are my palms. I must have scratched them open pretty good on the rough asphalt.

"She doesn't need a doctor. I'll bring her back to my place and clean her up."

"Are you sure about that?" Parker interjects. "You're not right in the head at the moment. I don't know if this is a good idea."

"Shut up," Warren closes his eyes, and his nostrils flare as he takes a calming breath. I can see the blood on his hands now. The vile violence he oozes makes it hard for me to breathe. I didn't think he cared about me, but clearly, he does.

"I'm fine," I whisper quietly, so quietly, I'm surprised he even heard me. "I want to go home with Warren."

"See, she is fine. I'll take her back to my house. You do something with him. I don't give a fuck what it is." Warren gestures to James' bloodied body.

Willow shakes her head, clearly not convinced, but she doesn't say anything and instead shoves up off the grass. Warren moves closer, his hands are on me in the next instant. Warmth courses through my veins at his touch. He picks me up like I weigh nothing and starts carrying me away from the scene.

His familiar scent invades my nostrils, and I suck in a greedy breath. Closing my eyes, I rest my head on Warren's shoulder and get lost in his presence. Never have I been happier to see him in my life.

13

WARREN

*H*arper is half asleep when I put her on my bed. Part of me wants to cover her up and let her sleep, but I resist, needing to get her cleaned up and taken care of first. Using caution so as not to cause her any more pain, I peel her jeans off and look at her battered knees. That fucking bastard. I grind my teeth together in rage. If I could've gotten away with it, I would've killed him for touching her.

Her skin is scraped up, but it's not deep, and nothing she needs to see a doctor for. I just need to clean and wrap it for the night. She'll have some aches and pains in the morning, but she's not going to die from her injuries.

"Don't move, I'm getting a first aid kit," I tell her as I get up and hurry into the bathroom. Quickly, I wash my hands, letting the fucker's blood from my knuckles run down the drain. I pull out the kit from underneath the sink and jog back into the room. She hasn't moved an inch, and I don't think it's because I told her to. I think she is still in shock.

Getting out the antiseptic and some cotton, I start cleaning her wounds. I make sure all the dirt is off before rubbing some

Neosporin on it and bandage it up. I'm so focused on my task that I don't realize Harper has been staring at me until I'm done with her knees.

"Let me see your hands," I ask her, but she still doesn't move. I don't like this. Her not moving or talking. It makes my stomach hurt, but most importantly, it makes me want to get back in my car, go find James and make good on ending his life.

That fucker... forcing air into my lungs, I calm myself.

Taking a seat next to her on the bed, I grab hold of each hand, inspecting the palms. They are just as bad as her knees, maybe even worse.

Fuck, who knew scrapes could look this bad.

"I'm gonna take your shirt off before I clean these," I tell her, and she nods. Well, that's progress. A nod is better than no response. I help her out of her shirt, taking her bra off while I'm at it. I cover her up with my blanket before she can get cold, and leave her hands out, resting on top of the comforter.

Then I repeat the whole cleaning and wrapping process on her hands. When I'm done with that, I slip out of my own clothes and slide into the bed next to her. She shudders when I pull her closer, but immediately after, she cuddles into my side, snuggling so deep I think she's trying to disappear.

"Can I stay with you?" she asks after a moment of silence.

"Of course." Does she think I'm about to kick her out and make her go back to her place after everything that happened tonight? I'm a bastard, but I'm not completely heartless.

"I... I... don't just mean today," she mumbles, her voice wrapped up in sleep, the same way my arms are wrapped around her.

It takes me a moment for her words to make sense in my mind. She isn't asking to stay the night, she's asking to stay for good, like move in. The thought is both exciting and shocking. I know she is just saying this because she is in shock. No way would she ask to stay if she was in her right mind. Not after everything I've done, everything she's said to me. I'm the last person she would come to for comfort or protection.

"You don't mean that. You're just vulnerable and scared right now. Go to sleep."

"I mean it..." She whispers, and I tuck her in a little closer to my chest.

"Okay, let's talk about it in the morning," I say softly. It's the softest I've spoken to her in years. With Harper in my arms, my heart can finally ease to a normal rhythm, and when I close my eyes, sleep easily finds me. At least for tonight, I'll pretend like the woman I've loved since I was a kid is mine.

∽

When I wake up, Harper is no longer curled up next to me. She's now sprawled out on top of me like I'm the mattress. With her head on my chest, her small body blankets mine, and I can't remember the last time I woke up feeling so content.

I lean down and kiss the top of her head, smelling the sweet scent of her shampoo. Her breath fans out against my skin evenly, and her eyes remain closed. I could watch her sleep like this all day, and I might. There is something so peaceful about having her here with me.

As I lie here, my eyes glued to the woman on top of me, I wonder if I could ever forgive her. Until now, the thought seemed outrageous. How could I ever forget what she did? But in the last twelve hours, I've realized like never before, how much of a hold she still has on me.

Will I ever be done with her? I don't think so, and if that's the case, what is our future going to look like if I don't forgive her?

My thoughts are interrupted when she stirs. Her body rubs against me like a kitten, her leg skimming over my already hardened cock. I've been hard for hours, aching with need, by watching her sleep. It gave me more satisfaction than anything else has before.

Opening her hazel eyes, she lifts her head from my chest and looks up at me. Then she lowers her head again, turning it so I can't see her expression. She buries her face back into my chest. Like it could save her from me.

"You regret what you asked me last night?"

"No, I do want to stay here."

"Why?"

"You know why."

"I need to hear you say it out loud."

She lifts her head again, and this time she stares me straight in the eyes. "Because it doesn't matter how much you act like a monster, or how badly you treat me. I still want you. And even though you've done a lot of shit to me, I still feel safe with you, and I know how fucked up that is. So, you don't have to rub it in my face. But it doesn't change anything. I want you, no matter what. Is that what you want to hear?"

"Yes," I shamelessly admit. "I like you weak for me, and I like knowing that you need me. It makes me feel..."

"Powerful. Like a king?" Harper answers before I can finish.

"Yes, but it makes me feel useful too. Like I have meaning to my life." I don't know why I'm confessing this to her. It doesn't change anything... *but maybe it can.* Maybe we can move on. A newfound excitement bursts through me. It won't be easy, not at all, but maybe I can put the past behind us. Maybe I can have Harper.

Harper makes a sour face at me, "What kind of meaning? Like the one you had with that girl in the hallway yesterday?"

I clench my jaw, of course, she's bringing that up. Then again, this is kind of my fault. My intention was for her to see me with another chick, and for her to assume that she wasn't the only one I was getting ass from, but I'm not going to lie. Letting Bridget paw at me, letting her think she even had a chance, it made me sick to my stomach.

"That's sounding a lot like jealousy, baby."

"I'm not jealous," she lifts her chin, fire dancing in her eyes. "It's just after your big, I'm yours, speech, I was surprised to see you with someone else."

"I told you that you are mine, not that I am yours." As soon as I say the words, I regret them. The pain in her face is so much of a reminder of my own that I can't stand it. Desperate to wipe that agony from her face, I continue, "You are cute when you are jealous though, and don't worry, you're the only one I'm fucking."

Shoving away from me, she winces, and I don't know if it's her knees and palms that are hurting her or my words. She grabs the blanket and pulls it to her chest covering her body, "You can say all you want that you don't care about me, that I don't mean anything to you, but you proved to me last night that I matter."

"How is that?" I tilt my head to the side and let my eyes roam over her. I want to peel that blanket back and kiss every inch of her silky-smooth skin.

"You saved me from James. You beat his ass, brought me back here, and took care of me. If that isn't compassion, then I don't know what is." She stares at me triumphantly, and she's right. I do care about her. I care about her too much, and that's the fucking problem here.

"James fucked with something that belongs to me, so he got his ass handed to him. Maybe I just wanted to make sure that my fuck doll was kept in one piece?" I lie through my teeth.

Harper rolls her eyes, seeing right through my deception, "Right, is that why you still haven't made a move to try and fuck me yet?"

"No matter what. You're mine, Harper. *Mine.*"

"Why do you want me to be yours so badly?" Her question catches me off guard. Of course, deep down, I already know the answer. The thing is, I don't want to admit it. Not to her or to myself.

"Maybe I do care about you... but I don't know what that means yet. I don't know if there will ever be an *us* again. I'll let you stay here with me, but I expect something out of the deal." I want to fuck her, rut into her like an animal, but I need to be gentle with her, at least right now. "Something tells me you won't have a problem giving it to me either."

Reaching for the blanket, I give it a tug, and unsurprisingly, she lets it go without a fight. Her cheeks turn a soft crimson, and her lips part, that pink tongue of hers darting out over her bottom lip.

"I want you," I purr softly.

"Like you wanted that other girl?" she whispers, and I feel the pain of her admission deep in my chest. I know confessing that I did it to make her jealous might make me weak, but after last night, the last thing I care about is letting her think I wanted someone else. The truth is, I can't stop thinking about her.

"The only one I want is you," I reply, moving closer to her.

She blinks, her pupils dilate, and she moves a little closer, seeking out the comfort of my body. Reaching for her, I hold her close and press soft kisses against her skin, her forehead, cheeks, and then down her chest. I want to worship the very ground she walks on. I want what we *could've* had, *should've* had, so badly, that I'm willing to forgive, but can I truly forget?

"Lie on your back. I want to remind you why you're mine, and that even though I'm a monster and beast, I can still use these same fingers and tongue that give you pain, to bring you pleasure." She doesn't fight me as I press a gentle hand to her chest. Instead, she falls back against the sheets and looks up at me.

Looking into her eyes, the entire world around us fades away. I forget about all my troubles, sorrows, and pain. There is just us, and nothing else. With a feverish, but tender need, I pepper kisses down the length of her body, moving until I reach her mound.

With a hand, I spread her legs, and they fall open, exposing her pretty pussy to me. Her folds are already glistening with arousal, and I swallow the groan down that was forming in my throat. My mouth waters, and it's like no matter how much I try and satiate my appetite for her, I can never get enough. I'm always hungry, always ready for more. No one and nothing else will ever satisfy my need like Harper does.

Falling to my stomach, I slide my hands under her ass and bring her pussy to my face.

"Warren," she squeals, and I smile joyfully. It reminds me of all the times when we were kids, and I would do whatever I could to make her smile and laugh.

"Let me feast," I growl and dive into her pussy like it's an Olympic pool. I show no mercy when it comes to curbing my needs. I lick and taste her like it's my last time. Like I'll never be given another chance.

Her hands move into my hair, tugging on the strands, each tug sends a pulse of red-hot pleasure straight to my cock. Licking her from top to bottom, I pay special attention to her clit as I bury my face between her folds. I suck and nibble on the diamond-hard bud, before dipping my tongue inside her tight entrance. She starts to grind her pussy against my face, and I let her, licking her right where she needs me most, in her warm, pink, center.

When she starts to wither against the sheets, I know she's close.

"Mmmm..." I growl into her folds and pinch her clit between my teeth. I do this a couple more times, and I'm rewarded with a deep throaty moan. A few seconds later, she explodes, her release gushing into my mouth. I lap every sweet drop up before pulling away, then I sit up, spread her thighs real wide, and drag the head of my cock to her entrance.

"You're on birth control, right?"

"Yes, I told you the other day," she says, her tone needy.

"Good, 'cause I'm about to blow a fat load in you." I'm tempted to slam into her but instead ease in, watching as her eyes roll to the back of her head with pleasure, her tight little pussy still convulses around my cock, barely allowing me entrance.

"Mine," I growl as I possessively move in and out of her. My hands grip onto her hips, holding her in place, but no matter how much I tell myself to be gentle in touching her, I can't. I need to make sure she knows she's mine, that if anyone fucks with her, they're fucking with me. "You have always belonged with me," I hiss, pumping in and out of her. She mewls, her pink lips part, and she gasps as I swivel my hips, my cock grazing her g-spot.

I can't get enough of her, and it's like no matter how badly the downfall will be, no matter how much it's going to hurt when it all falls apart, I'll go through the pain even for a tiny slice of heaven.

"I'm...I'm coming..." Harper whimpers, her big hazel eyes pierce mine, and when we're like this, I can feel how vulnerable and fragile she is, and if I had my way, I'd have her like this forever, but I can't.

Wanting to feel closer to her and be deeper inside her, I pick her up and haul her to my chest. The movement sends her over the edge, and as she falls apart in my arms, I thrust upward, her tight channel squeezing my own release from my balls. Without warning, I start coming, filling her with my sticky release.

Chest to chest, I can feel our pulses matching in beat. Hearts slamming against hearts. I want this forever with her, but again I'm reminded of our past. Forgive, but forget? I don't know. I don't know if I can let the pain of her betrayal go. Deep down, I know I still love her. I know she is it for me, but...

Staring at each other, our eyes locked together, her arms wrapped around my neck. Nothing in this world could ruin this moment, nothing. Then a knock sounds against the door, and for a moment, I think I'm hearing things.

The doorknob jiggles, and I don't know what to think, or even do.

"Open the door, son," my father's stern voice filters through the door. What the hell is he doing here? I blink the confusion from my eyes and watch in horror as Harper scurries off my lap. She grabs the blanket and wraps it around herself as if that's going to make her disappear from the room.

She looks like she might throw up, and that's not surprising; my father has that impact on people. I contemplate telling her to go hide in the bathroom but decide against it. I don't care what my father has to say. Most likely, he won't even remember her.

Moving off the bed, I pull on a pair of shorts from the floor and walk over to the door. I give Harper one last look before I undo the lock and open the door.

14

HARPER

I still can't believe I asked him to let me stay here. He was right, last night I was just scared and vulnerable. I would have said anything to make myself feel even a little safe. But the truth is, I really do want to stay here and not just because I'm scared. I want him, I want him like I've always wanted him. Seeing how Warren took care of me last night and how he treated me this morning... I think he still wants me too. The only thing standing in our way now is whatever he thinks I did all those years ago. Staring into each other's eyes, I don't think the moment can get any better. I want to tell him that whatever he thinks I did, I didn't do but a knock sounds against the door, followed by a deep voice.

"Open the door, son." It takes me a moment to digest what is happening and who is on the other side of that door, but when I do, I scurry off of Warren's lap and wrap myself up in the blanket. *His father is here.* I think I'm going to puke. That man has always given me the creeps. I don't think I've ever seen a smile on his face.

Moving slowly, Warren gets up from the bed and pulls on a

pair of shorts. He takes his time getting to the door and gives me a sympathetic look as he opens it. Readying myself, I'm fully prepared to jump up, put my clothes on, and run out of the room, but that would mean walking right past his father, and no way am I doing that right now.

Luckily, Warren steps into the doorway, shielding most of his father's view of me. In fact, he moves into the hall, closing the door almost completely behind him.

"Who is the girl?" is the first thing his father asks.

"No one, now what the hell do you want?" Warren goes on the defensive, and my stomach twists into an angry knot.

"You think you're a big man now? Need I remind you who bought this house, your car, and pays your tuition? Talk to me like I'm your father and not one of your damn friends."

There is a brief pause and then Warren speaks again, "What do you want, Dad?" This time, when he replies, he sounds bored rather than angry.

"Who is the girl?" There is a darkness in his father's voice, and I feel it in my soul. It slithers over my skin, my arms, and chest, wrapping around my throat like a snake.

"I already told you, no one."

Does his father make a habit of doing this with all the girls Warren sleeps with?

"Let's see," he says in a condescending tone. In a flash, the door is shoved open, and Warren's father's eyes collide with mine. "She is a no one all right. I thought you'd know better than to mess around with that whore again."

Whore? Anger pulses through my veins, and I bite the inside of my cheek until I taste the coppery tang of blood.

Warren stares at me with sorrow in his eyes before grabbing the door and pulling it closed. In an instant, I'm left alone with my thoughts again. Footsteps sound against the wooden floor, moving away from the bedroom. Part of me wants to get up and listen, but part of me doesn't. I don't want to hear what his father has to say about me. I know I'm not a whore. I've only ever been with Warren, but that doesn't change the fact that I want to know what he's saying about me.

As I sit there wrapped in the blanket, I start to shiver. Even though I'm engulfed in warmth, I still feel cold, so cold. Why does Warren's father think so shitty of me? Is it because we come from different classes? Because he is rich and I'm poor? Is it because my parents used to work for him before he rudely fired them?

All these questions burn through me, stoking the angry fire in my chest. As I wait for Warren to return, I go to his dresser and find something of his I can wear. Careful not to rip any of the bandages Warren put on me, I slip into a long sleeve shirt and sweatpants, which I have to roll to keep from falling down. Finally dressed, I feel much better, and a little less vulnerable. When Warren finally comes back into the room, he looks pissed, and I'm not sure if his anger is directed at his father or me.

"I'm sorry about him," he mutters, shoving a frustrated hand through his hair. "He shouldn't have called you that."

"I don't care what he says or thinks about me," I give him the honest truth. There is something else that affected me much more than being called a whore. Going on the defense isn't going to help me, I know this, but I'm still burning mad. "You told him I was no one to you."

Warren's face falls, "I don't want my father to know who I care about. He'll just use it against me." His tone is already a little calmer as he sits down next to me on the bed. Reaching for my hand, he covers my cold one with his much larger, warm one.

"Why did your father call me a whore?" I ask. Even though I'm not hurt by it, I'm still curious. As if my touch has suddenly burned him, he pulls away.

"Let's not talk about that today," he snaps. I sigh in frustration, but let it go because I really don't have the energy to fight with him right now.

"Can we just crawl back into bed and sleep all day?"

"I don't know if there will be a lot of sleeping if I crawl back in that bed with you," he smirks, and I'm glad I didn't push the question. "How about I cook us something, and we can be lazy and lounge on the couch all day?"

My eyes light up, "Yes, let's do that."

Warren makes good on making us some food. He pops two pizzas in the oven while I try and find something to watch on TV. It's been a while since I watched anything, between school and the fact that we could never afford it growing up, I don't really know what's decent to watch. Tossing the remote down, I all but jump out of my skin when the front door opens, and Warren's roommates come stomping into the house.

"Is that pussy or pizza I smell?" Cameron chuckles.

"It's going to be a broken nose, and a busted lip you'll smell if you don't shut the fuck up," Warren growls as he appears in the living room.

Easton laughs, and walks into the living room, with Cameron trailing not far behind.

"Dude, you have got to learn to take a joke," Cameron taunts.

Warren shakes his head and takes the seat next to me while Cameron goes left, and Easton goes right, leaving us in the middle of the two of them.

I can already feel how tense Warren is, his arm wrapping

around me possessively. Does he think these two are going to steal me away or something?

"How is Harper doing?" Easton teases, giving me a wink. I'm not sure if I should reply or if that would set him off, so instead, I say nothing.

I run my finger over the edge of the bandaged palm absentmindedly, when Easton's eyes catch on the movement. He looks down and stops at my bandages. "What happened to your hands?"

"Nothing," I murmur, not wanting to be reminded of last night, but when I lower my gaze, I catch sight of his hands. His knuckles are swollen, and the skin is broken in some places. It looks like he got into a fight, even though his face looks fine, so maybe the fight was one-sided. "What happened to your hands?"

"Nothing," he echoes my own word, and I decide to be satisfied with that answer just like he was with mine.

"Don't you two fucks have anything else to do? Girls to stalk or something?"

Easton taps on his chin with his finger, he's handsome, but not in the same way Warren is. He's more rugged and unkempt.

"Ahhh, let me think, no. We love annoying you."

"Why have us as roommates if you hate us so much?" Cameron snickers and the only place this conversation is going is to the jail because Warren is going to beat the piss out of these guys if they don't go away. I don't know what it is about him, but Warren is beyond territorial.

"I'm telling you now..." Warren clenches and unclenches his fist.

"Warren..." I whisper into his ear and place my hand

against his thigh. "Maybe they want to watch a movie with us? They are your roommates."

Easton and Cameron say nothing, and Warren stares at me for a long moment, before reaching for the remote. Releasing a sigh, I know I've won this fight. As he finds something to watch, I snuggle into his side.

Warren turns on something called *Game of Thrones*, and the guys immerse themselves in it. After a short while, I start to fall asleep, but I'm startled awake when they start talking. I'm drifting in and out of sleep, but I'm pretty sure I hear them saying something about a girl who saw them do something.

Warren tells them to shut up and runs his fingers through my hair.

Easton and Cameron continue to talk, but eventually, their voices get quieter, telling me they've left the room. Now that we're alone, I start to sink deeper like a stone sinking into the dark waters.

Just before I fall off the deep end, I swear I hear Warren say... *I love you,* and somehow, that tells me everything is going to be okay. Even though his dad hates me, and we haven't exactly been on great terms, I know Warren wants me. He's always wanted me, and maybe this is our chance, our chance at forever.

15

WARREN

We walk up to the apartment building Harper used to stay in. The thought of her sleeping in this dump still enrages me. I am so glad she hasn't been here in over a week. Instead, she's been staying at my place, in my bed with me... where she belongs. Where she's always belonged.

My phone buzzes in my pocket, and without even looking, I know who it is. My father has been calling and texting me nonstop, wanting me to come to the house and talk about Harper. He doesn't want me to see her, thinks I'm making a mistake. He says it's because he is worried about me getting hurt again, but part of me knows damn well that he thinks she is beneath our standards. He thinks I should date someone in our class. What he doesn't realize is that Harper has more class in her little finger than most of the girls here.

"You okay?" Harper asks, holding out her now healed hand to me.

I take it before answering, "Yeah, I'm good. I'm just glad

you don't live here anymore. Let's get all of your stuff, so we don't have to come back here ever again."

"Fine by me. I like it at your place better... someone cooks for me there."

"And I like you at my place 'cause that means someone keeps my bed warm for me," I tease, making her giggle. We walk up the stairs, the sound of her laughter still echoing through the sad-looking staircase.

When we get to her room, she gets out the key and opens her small apartment. The moment she steps in, I can feel her tense up next to me. She doesn't like being here, and again, guilt hits me. I sent her back here the night after I fucked her. After I already knew what a shitty place this is. Even knowing that someone broke in here, I made her sleep here again.

"Are you sure you're okay?" she asks, concern for *me* lacing her voice, and the irony is not lost on me.

"Yeah, let's just get this over with, and just so you know, you are never going to stay in a place like this again."

"If you say so," she gives me a tiny smile before turning away from me to pack up her stuff. She gets a suitcase out of the wall closet and places it on her bed. She doesn't have many clothes. In fact, the entire contents of her dresser fits into her one suitcase. I zip it up and put it beside the door for now.

I try and help her as much as I can without getting in the way, but there really isn't much for me to do. When she goes into the attached bathroom, I start looking around for stuff to pack.

The kitchen, if you can even call it that, has nothing in it that we can't buy her new. Plus, she has everything she needs at my house. No use for rusted pots and pans and mismatched cups and plates. Sweeping the room again, I catch sight of a pink box peeking out from under the bed. Curiously, I walk over to the bed and sit on the edge of it. It squeaks under my weight, and I reach down and pull out the box. I take the lid off slowly. I feel like a kid sneaking downstairs to open a Christmas present three days early.

I mean what could really be in this box…

As soon as the lid is pulled off enough for me to reveal the contents, I freeze. Hell, I almost drop the box when I see the small assortment of vibrators inside it. There isn't anything crazy in there, but still, I'm somewhat shocked to find a box of vibrators under my sweet Harper's bed.

"Are you snooping?" Harper appears back in the open space.

Like a kid caught with his hand in the cookie jar, I slam the box shut and sit it on the ground in front of me, as if I never touched it at all. Harper starts laughing, and I won't lie; she looks, so sexy smiling.

"What, you've never seen a vibrator before?"

"I'm just surprised," I shrug, doing my best not to make a big deal out of it.

"Why? I didn't have a boyfriend after you, but I still have… you know… *needs.*"

"Oh, I know your *needs,* all right," I smirk. I know her needs very well. She was made for me and me for her.

She walks over to the bed where I'm sitting. Her fingers trailing over my shoulders, and she sits down on my lap. "Maybe you can show me how well you know?"

She doesn't have to ask me twice. Pouncing like a wild animal, I have her on her back in a second flat, my hand wrapped around her delicate throat. I don't squeeze because the point isn't to show her I can hurt her. I want control.

My other hand disappears into her jeans, finding its way into her panties and between her thighs with ease, her sweet arousal already forming there.

Her eyes flutter closed, and she lets out a soft moan. I can feel the sound vibrating under my touch. I'm going to take that as a yes. With a smile on my lips, I release her throat and press kisses against it, loving the feeling of having her beneath me.

I imagine this is how it always would've been with us, had we made it to this point. Teasing her entrance with my fingers, I dip one digit inside her and then pull it back out. I do this a few times, noticing how much wetter she gets each time I slide back in.

"Stop teasing me," Harper groans in displeasure and takes her own hand and places it over mine. "If you won't please me, then I'll do it myself."

The bite of her words sink into my flesh, almost as if she's bitten me, and I swear my cock gets ten times harder. Pleasure swells in my chest, and I pull off her pants and panties in one move.

"Show me," I order, pulling back just enough to get a full view, wanting to see her finger herself.

Harper's cheeks turn a soft pink, and she bites her bottom lip in a seductive way that has me wanting to take that lip and bite on it, make it bleed.

"I've never done this with someone watching," she tells me shyly, and that turns me on more. At least I get one first.

"Good. I want you to be all mine. Finger your pussy, rub your clit, make yourself come..." I say, swallowing down my need to go to her when her finger starts to rub against her folds. Her eyes remain on mine while I look between her pussy and her face, becoming completely mesmerized by her.

Spreading her legs wider, her fingers start to move faster. One digit slips into her tight channel, and with the palm of her hand, she rubs her clit. Fuck, I wish my cock was her finger right now.

I make quick work of my pants and boxers, so I can fist my length in my hand. Using my thumb, I spread the pre-cum that beads the tip over the head.

Her head falls back against the mattress, and a throaty moan that I feel deep in my toes slips from her throat.

"Stop," I growl and march over to her. "If you're going to come, it's going to be on my cock, and only on my cock." Barely restraining my need for her, I grab her and flip her over. She doesn't make a sound, and instead shoves her ass into the air, wiggling it at me. Doesn't she know if you provoke the bull, you get the horns?

Crawling up onto the bed, I situate myself behind her and bring the head of my cock to her entrance. As hard as it is, and it's really fucking hard, pun intended, I slide into her as slow as I can, watching as she swallows every thick inch of my cock.

My balls press against her ass, and I swear we both let out a sigh that is filled with both contentment and desire. After a beat, I place both hands on her perfect hips and start fucking her like there is no tomorrow.

Harper becomes a sexy lioness then, pushing back against me, fucking me as I fuck her, and I've never felt so much being exchanged between two people.

"You feel like heaven, like fucking home..." The words come out hoarse, and I shouldn't say them, but I can't hold them back. Not now, and maybe not ever again. My feelings for her are only growing, blossoming with each new day.

"Warren, oh, god..." She cries, and it's music to my ears. I've never heard a cry so fucking sweet.

"What do you need?" I purr, trailing a hand up her spine as I continue to jackhammer inside her.

"You. Harder. Faster. I just need you," she pants against the mattress, and I let my hand move to the back of her neck. Brushing her silky hair away, I maintain a firm grip and take control completely, holding her down while I own her pussy like it was meant to be owned.

Faster and harder, I thrust, swiveling my hips to make the head of my cock touch that sweet spot that I know will have her gushing all over me.

"Oh, yes... yes..." Harper whimpers, her words muffled, but I can still make them out.

"Don't fight it. Come on my cock," I thrust my hips faster, listening to the sound of our skin slapping together, and watch as our juices drip down my length and gather at my balls.

Harper starts to come then; her channel squeezes the life right out of me. Once she starts to fall apart, my own release begins to crest. I come like I've never come before, my cock spasming inside of her as I paint her womb with my sticky release.

Sagging against her, I press a kiss to her clammy forehead. I'm falling for her, falling deeper and deeper, and soon there won't be any saving me. My heart is growing again, beating stronger, and if everything falls apart again... I can't even think about that right now. Easing out of Harper, I grab a couple of tissues from her nightstand that still hasn't been packed and clean the insides of her thighs. I can feel her eyes on me the entire time, watching my every movement.

"Are you okay?" she asks for the tenth time, and I wonder if she can see through my mask, see how much I still fucking want her and how much it's killing me to deal with all these thoughts and feelings.

Not wanting to ruin what we have, I nod, "Yes, I'm fine, babe, now stop asking me every five seconds if I'm okay. If I wasn't, I would tell you," I lie, because I'm not about to tell her what's wrong. I don't want to talk about it. All I want to do is forget and move on. I don't want to continue to relive the past.

16

HARPER

Warren has been acting strange lately, or at least stranger than usual. When he walks me to class today, Easton is already there, and, of course, he waves and smiles at me. I return the smile and wave before turning back to say goodbye to Warren, who is staring daggers into Easton's head. I don't understand his need to be territorial.

"Hey, I was just saying hi," I say softly. "I thought we were past this?"

"I don't care. I told you not to talk to him, and I'm tired of you doing whatever the hell you want. You know Easton pisses me off, you know his stupid antics make me lose my mind, but yet, you feed right into it." Anger rushes off of him in waves.

Unable to hold in my own anger, I lash out at him, "I don't do anything. He's your roommate, and I'm your... well, I don't even know what I am to you. All you keep saying is that I'm yours, but you're not mine. So, I don't know what that means, but it surely doesn't mean you have to piss in a circle around me."

The look in his eyes is feral, and his hands curl into tight fists, "You'll regret talking to me like this. You belong to me, Harper. When I tell you to do something, you do it. Maybe I need to remind you of that."

Without so much as a goodbye, he turns and walks away, leaving me to simmer in my own anger. Gritting my teeth, I stomp into the classroom and take my usual seat, tugging my books out of my bag.

"Everything okay?" Easton asks as I situate my stuff.

"No, everything is not okay," I growl. I don't understand him. We never discussed what we are or if we are exclusive. Which doesn't even matter because all I did was say hi. I can't wave at someone like Easton, who I share a class with? What am I supposed to do? Look the other way when he enters the room?

"Warren's a tough cookie sometimes. When I first met him, I thought he was a douchebag. He fucked girls like it was a competitive sport, then you came into his world, and everything changed."

"Great, he fucked every girl in this school, but I can't wave at you." I snort. "Whatever, it doesn't matter. We're just mad at each other and need some space." Easton nods like he understands, but I doubt he knows a damn thing about relationships. Walking away, he takes his own seat, and the professor starts discussing the reading material from over the weekend.

I'm knee-deep in notes, absorbing every single thing the professor says when the door to the room opens, and a woman pops her head inside. The professor stops speaking and walks over to greet her. They exchange a short conversation before the woman steps completely into the room. Confused, I set my pen down and wait for something to happen.

"Is there a Harper Martin in this class?" the woman asks.

I swallow thickly and raise my hand like a small child. At the movement, her eyes clash with mine.

"Hello, Miss Martin, I need you to please come with me." I nod and stand on shaky legs, shoving my stuff into my bag. A knot of worry tightens in my gut. Did something happen to my parents? I don't know who this woman is or why she's asking me to leave, but something tells me it's not good. Tossing my backpack over my shoulder, I walk down the aisle, listening to all the whispers as I walk by.

When I reach the woman, I look over my shoulder at Easton, who's looking at me with the same expression I'm wearing. *Confusion.* The lady opens the door and ushers me out into the hall, following closely behind me.

"Is everything okay?" I ask.

"We will talk about it once we reach the admissions building." Even though I have a thousand and one questions, I keep my lips closed and follow her to the building. What could possibly be going on?

When we finally reach her office, I take a seat in the chair in front of her long wooden desk. A metal plaque is sitting on the smooth surface, reading Mrs. Jensen, financial aid. Only then does it occur to me that this may have to do with my scholarship.

Taking the seat opposite me, she crosses her hands in front of her and looks me straight in the eyes, disappointment reflecting back at me.

"Do you have any idea why I have called you into my office?"

I shake my head because I'm smart enough not to question until I have all the answers.

She nods her head, "Blackthorn was recently made aware by a concerned patron that you're not living in the dorms but are receiving payments for housing through the school. If you don't live on campus and are receiving payments specifically for that expense, you are committing fraud."

My mouth pops open and closes and then opens again. This is worse than I thought, so much worse.

"Effective immediately, you will no longer receive housing payment, and furthermore, we need you to repay that money as soon as possible. If you fail to repay the money, we will be forced to pull your scholarship."

Shock, rage, dread, and sadness all engulf me at once. Through the fog of emotions surrounding me, one name pops into my head. *Warren.* He did this. He threatened me time and time again, and now he finally did it, and all over what? Me waving at Easton?

"I don't have that kind of money. I'm using the money to rent a cheaper place off-campus and the rest of the money to pay for food and books. Surely, there is something that we can do to fix this?" I reply desperately, pinning Mrs. Jensen with a pleading stare.

Apparently, she's not impressed by my admission, either that or she simply doesn't care.

"The way to fix this would've been to have been staying in the dorms all along. I've already discussed this with the other school board members, and they've decided that you can either pay the payments back, or you can forfeit your scholarship. Might I add, that you're lucky to be given a chance out of this and that the school is not pressing charges for fraud."

Tears sting my eyes... he got what he wanted. He got rid of me. I was so stupid to think that Warren and I were moving past whatever it was that was eating him.

"I'm sorry, I don't know how to pay back the money, and I

don't know how to live on campus. I would have no money for books or food or anything else for that matter."

"Look, the only thing I can do for you is set up a payment plan for the housing money you owe. It's only for one semester. It's not that much."

Not to you, maybe. Unsure what to tell her, I just stare at my hands in my lap.

"I'll tell you what," she continues, "how about I give you until tomorrow to figure it out?"

"Okay," I agree, knowing damn well that there is nothing to figure out. I pretty much just lost my scholarship. Lost everything I worked hard for. "Thanks," I mumble, before getting up and heading out of her office.

As soon as I'm out the door, the tears start to fall. With blurry vision, I start walking away from the building and off the campus. There's no reason for me to go back to class. No reason for me to study or think about tests and homework. The only two things I need to worry about now is where the hell I'm going to live and how the hell I'm going to pay for it.

Everything I worked for is gone... gone.

∽

"WHAT DO you mean they want the money back? Who cares where you live?" Valerie asks.

"Because if I'd lived on the campus, I guess the money ends up back in their pockets somehow," I shrug. "Either way, it doesn't matter. I broke the rules, and now I have to deal with it. Are you sure I can stay here for a while?"

"Yes, I'm sure. As long as you want," she reassures me. I couldn't bring myself to go to my parents' place. I don't want to face them yet. Face the disappointment that I know they will have when they hear I fucked up, and I definitely won't go back to Warren. Which left me with Valerie as the only other place I could go. It might not be the best choice in the long run, but it's the best for me right now.

"Thanks, Val. I mean it."

"It's okay. I owe you anyway. For all the times I've been a major bitch to you."

"I'm not going to argue with that."

"I know, and I'm sorry. Maybe this can be our new beginning? You and me, roommates. It doesn't sound that bad."

"Yeah, not too bad. So, are you still working at the diner?"

"Sure do, got a raise too, and tips are great."

"Maybe I could start working there? So I can help out with rent and stuff?" I'm going to have to get used to a minimum wage job, so why not start at a diner? I'm sure the pay won't be that great starting out, but I can get tips which should cover it.

"Ah, well... I-I don't think they need anyone right now," she tells me, suddenly sounding nervous, her eyes darting around the room. "We're pretty well staffed. Should be like that for a while too. You could definitely look for a job elsewhere though."

"Oh, okay..." I guess she doesn't want me to work with her. Or maybe she thinks I won't be able to do the job well? Whatever it is, if Val won't help me find a job, I can do it on my own.

"I have to get to work. Working the graveyard shift, but you're free to stay for as long as you would like." I give her a tight-lipped smile and take a seat on the couch. I guess I'll sleep here for the night, and just take it day by day.

"Thanks again, Val. I might not be here in the morning. Going to try and start job hunting early." Valerie nods as she reaches the door. She looks a little more dolled up than I would expect a waitress to be, but if it gets her good money, then I get it. You have to do what you have to do. As soon as she's gone and I'm left alone with my thoughts, I look around the small apartment and am reminded of how much it looks like mine did.

I have nothing now. No scholarship, no home, nothing, and all because I believed that things were different between Warren and me now. Fishing my phone out of my pocket, I power the thing down before *he* can call me. I don't have it in me to fight with him right now.

Nothing he says can fix this. He threatened me, warned me, and I basically gave him the ammunition he needed earlier today.

Stupid me. Stupid heart. I should've used my brain. The tears start to come then, and there isn't any way to stop them.

I gave my heart to Warren again, but this time he didn't just break it, he destroyed my life. He took everything from me.

17

WARREN

I kicked myself in the ass the entire time Harper was in class. I never should've spoken to her like that. Like a territorial asshole. I know she's mine, and she knows she's mine, and yet, I had to go and make a stupid comment.

Leaning against a tree outside the science lab, I wait for Harper to be done with her class. An apology already sitting on the tip of my tongue. Students start to filter out of the building. But Harper isn't one of them. The moment I see Easton walk out, his eyes meet mine, and I know something is wrong.

Pushing away from the tree, I meet him halfway. "What's wrong? Where is Harper?"

Easton shakes his head, "One of the financial aid people came and got her out of class. She never came back. I figured she would have called you by now."

Worry bubbles within my gut. "Shit. How do you know it was financial aid? Who was it?"

"Brian told me who she was," Easton shrugs. "I don't know

her name, but she had brown hair, glasses and was wearing a gray suit."

Spinning around on my heels, I sprint away before Easton has even finished speaking. The jog, well, more like run, to the admin building seems to take forever, and when I arrive, I ask for financial aid at the front desk. A middle-aged woman points me in the right direction with a questioning brow. There are three offices for financial aid, but only one is a woman, so I decide that it has to be her.

I knock but don't wait for her to say anything. Pushing the door open, I walk into the office at the same time.

"Excuse you," she half yells while pushing up from her desk. The woman looks exactly like Easton described her, so I don't ask her anything but the most important question.

"Why did you pull Harper Martin out of class?" I take another step and stop right in front of her desk, pinning her with a dark stare.

"And you are? Legally, I can't give you answers to questions like that."

"I'm her boyfriend," I answer without thinking. It sounds weird saying those words again, but I don't have time to dwell on the thought.

"If that's so, then you know where she lives?"

"With me."

"And, are you aware of the fact that Miss Martin is receiving money to live on-campus?"

Fuck, so they found out.

"So what? Who cares? And how do you even know about this?" Since I have her talking, I might as well keep getting whatever information I can out of her.

"It doesn't matter who made us aware of it, what matters is that it happened and needed to be addressed immediately." I don't know if she mentioned a *who* on purpose, but either way, I know someone ratted her out, and I have a good idea about who it might be. I'll deal with him later though, because right now I have to fix this. Fix this big-ass mess for Harper.

"What do you mean addressed? What's going to happen? Did she lose her scholarship?"

"Not yet, but she will if she doesn't pay back the money, and she won't be receiving any further payments for housing. So even if she does manage to pay the school back, she's going to need to find a place to live."

Without a second thought, I pull out my wallet and grab my credit card, throwing it down onto the shiny wooden desk between us.

"Here, I'll pay for it."

"Okay," the lady chirps, taking my card without question. I guess they don't care where the money comes from as long as it's paid. She runs the card, and I sign the receipt and put my card back in my wallet before heading out. I don't even think about how much money I spent, or what is happening between us. Right now, the only thing of importance to me is ensuring that Harper can continue her education.

In the beginning, I wanted her gone, but now... I just... I need her close, need to know she's okay.

Pulling the office door shut behind me, I tug my phone out of my pocket right away. Dialing Harper's number, I hold the phone to my ear just to be met by the sound of her voicemail. *Fuck*. Squeezing the phone so tightly, I fear the device might crumble under the pressure of my grip.

She turned her fucking phone off... again.

Acid burns up my throat and panic grips me. Even as angry as I am, the worry of her leaving is worse. Where the hell did she go? What is she thinking? *Fuck*, I know exactly what she is thinking. She blames me. She thinks I did this, just like I threatened I would.

On my way to my car, I call Valerie's phone just to get her voicemail too. I don't think she is there anyway. There is only one place I can think of to go, and that's her parents' house. I find the address she gave me before and put it in my GPS. Ten minutes later, I'm on my way, hoping that it's not too late.

How could I fuck this up? I should have already paid the stupid housing money. I should have told her that I wanted her to stay, that I would never tell the university about this. But my stupid head got in the way. I wanted to have something to hold against her, and all because I was scared that she would leave me if I didn't.

I only get about halfway to Harper's parents' house before my phone starts to ring. I grab it from the passenger seat, surprised to see Valerie's name light up the screen.

Answering, I say, "Hello."

"Did you rat out Harper to the school?" Valerie's accusing voice comes through the line. Caught off-guard but totally expecting it, I tell her the truth.

"No, I fucking didn't. Do you know where she is?"

"Yes..." She pauses, and I wait for the *but* to come, "She's at my place. I told her she can stay with me, but I kinda don't want her to stay. You know, with my job and all. It won't take her long to figure out I don't work at a diner."

Valerie is still talking while I make a U-turn at the next road.

"Send me your address, and I'll be there in thirty minutes." I punch the gas and squeeze the steering wheel in my hand.

"Fine, I'm on my way to work now. Can you maybe not tell her that I called you? I don't want her to be mad at me."

"Yeah, yeah... I get it, you don't want her to know what kind of person you really are."

"It's not like that, Warren," Valerie huffs.

"Send me the address. I won't tell her your secret; you can do that." Hanging up the phone, I start back in the direction of Blackthorn. After a few minutes, a text comes through with the address, and I punch it into the GPS on my phone.

The entire way back to Harper, I contemplate what I'm going to say and how I'm going to say it. I can't imagine what she is thinking right now. How upset she is, how shitty she thinks of me. Anger surges through me, and I hit the steering wheel with my hand, needing to lash out at something.

As the miles dwindle down, a nervous knot forms in my gut, and by the time I pull into the apartment complex, I'm a wreck. I park the car and look up at the building. It's similar to the one Harper lived in before, which only enrages me more. I told her she would never stay in a place like this again, and I meant it.

Getting out of the SUV, I walk across the parking lot, and up the front steps. There is no buzzer at the front door, so I go right in. I have to climb two flights of stairs and follow the long hallway toward Valerie's apartment number.

When I reach it, I let out a harsh breath and try to get my anger and breathing under control. I'm so fucking angry that someone did this to her. Yes, I had threatened to do it, but that was before everything happened.

Making a fist, I beat it against the wooden door.

Nothing.

I repeat the action, a little harder this time.

"Open the door, Harper. I know you're in there."

A second later, I can hear footsteps coming toward the

door. "Go away, Warren. I hate you, and I never want to see you again."

"Too bad. Open the fucking door, or I'll kick it in." I don't bother hiding my irritation. All I need is to have her in my arms, to tell her what happened, that I didn't do it. That will ease the anger, the madness threatening to overtake me.

"No," she replies, and I scrub a frustrated hand down my face. I doubt anyone would bat an eye if I started to kick in this door. Again, the neighborhood is shit, and the door is flimsy enough that it wouldn't take much effort.

"Harper," I warn. "I'm going to kick in the fucking door, and then Valerie's going to be pissed. Open it or make me go through it. Either way, I'm going to get my hands on you."

A second later, I hear the lock disengaging, and the door opens up a sliver, Harper's sleepy face fills the small space.

"Please, go away. You've already ruined everything, taken everything from me. What more could you want? Did you come here to embarrass me further? To break my heart all over again?" She sounds as defeated as I feel, and all I want to do is wrap her up in my arms, but I doubt she would let me touch her right now, not without lashing out like a feral cat at me.

"Let me in," I order, and take a step forward.

"No," she shakes her head.

"Okay," I shrug, and then rush forward, shoving the door open. She stumbles back and almost falls on her ass, but I grab her arm in time to steady her. She tries to shrug me off, but I don't let her. Never letting go, I close the door behind me.

"Why can't you just leave me alone?"

"You know why, and I wasn't the one who told the school about you living off-campus."

"Yeah, right. Of course, you didn't. You were only the one

threatening to do so for weeks." She waves her hands around like she doesn't know what to do with them, and she somehow needs to let the anger out. "Now you've got what you wanted, I'm gone. They are going to take my scholarship—"

"No, they won't. I paid back what you owed. Your scholarship is fine." My words have the desired effect, and she stops moving around. Her arms fall to the side of her body.

"You did, what?" she asks, her eyes wide.

"Yes, I told you, it wasn't me. I don't want you to leave..." I'm close to telling her why I don't want her to leave, why I would do anything to keep her close, but my stupid brain keeps getting in the way of pouring my heart out.

"What's the catch? What do I need to do for you in return?" Even though her reaction is completely justified, it still makes me angry. Maybe more so at myself.

"I need your complete obedience in all matters," I half-joke. Her mouth pops open, and I know she is about to start yelling at me, but I cut her off before it starts. "I'm joking. There is no catch."

"Warren... I can't do this. Where am I supposed to stay? I was paying for food and books with the leftover money. Without it, I have nothing."

"You will stay with me, and I'll give you anything else you need. You don't have to worry about this. Just pack your stuff and let's get out of here."

For a long moment, she just stares at me, I don't know if she expects me to say anything else and if she does, I don't know what she wants me to say.

"You aren't serious?" Her face twists into this strange look. It's both fear and joy. "Wait, you are."

"Let's go, Harper. I hate that you're back in the same situation as before, and on top of that, I need to do some investigating and find out who the hell did this."

"You don't have to help me. I can figure it out myself..." She stubbornly states, but I'm not having it. Grabbing her by the chin, I tilt her face to mine.

"I'll do whatever I fucking want, and because I *want* to help, I will. Now, please, stop being stubborn, grab your shit and let's leave."

Harper's lips form into a flat line, and it looks like she might fight me some more. My cock comes to life at the thought. I'll gladly take her over my knee and spank her ass until there isn't a lick of defiance left in her. Shockingly, she pulls from my hand, grabs her backpack off the couch, and slips her shoes on before walking back over to me.

"Ready," she murmurs.

I nod and grab her hand, tugging her out of the room and closing the door behind us. We walk down to the car in silence, even though I'm boiling over with anger and a need to unleash it. As soon as I have Harper in the car, I pull my phone out and walk around and get into the driver's side. Before I even start driving, I dial my father's number.

"Son," his voice meets my ear.

"Why did you do it? Just tell me," I growl, strangling the steering wheel with my free hand.

"Do what?" He plays dumb, which only makes me burn hotter.

"I'm not a fucking idiot. How did you find out about Harper staying off-campus, and why the fuck did you go to the school with the information?"

Silence. Nothing but silence greets me, and that's all the answer I need.

"Stay the fuck out of my shit and leave Harper alone."

"Do you really think a girl like her is at a university like Blackthorn to get an education? She is there for one thing only, to find a rich guy and use him. Probably trying to get knocked up." I press my phone closer to my ear.

"You know nothing about her," I growl into the phone, hoping that Harper didn't hear what he just said.

"I know enough. She's no good for you. She is going to use you like she did before. Mark my words. She will destroy you. You deserve better, and if I can get rid of her, then I will."

"Leave. Her. The. Fuck. Alone." I project each word into the speaker with a harshness that I'm sure even he can feel.

I'm done fucking around. Harper is mine, as she always has been. I don't care if her parents worked for mine. I don't care about our past anymore. All I care about is us and moving forward. I finally have her in my hands again, and nothing is going to ruin this for us.

"You're making a mistake, Warren. A huge fucking mistake."

"No, you are. Leave her alone." I hang up the phone and toss it over my shoulder, damn near swerving off the road in the process. Forcing air into my lungs, I focus all my attention on breathing, taking deep calming breaths. Looking over at Harper, I half expected her to be sank into her seat, fear in her hazel eyes, but that's the last thing I see.

Instead, I see something that I never thought I would see in her eyes again. *Love.*

It's such a profound feeling that it makes every other emotion inside of me dissolve into dust. Love? Could I love Harper again? Could I let go of everything, forget that she ever hurt me? I guess I'll have to decide because going against my father won't be easy, but it will be worth it if I get to have Harper.

18

HARPER

*E*verything goes back to normal, or as normal as it was before. I return to classes thanks to Warren, who is actually making an effort not to be so territorial when it comes to his friends. It seems like everything is going well, considering we are pretty much starting all over again. Well, apart from all the fighting he is doing with his father. That isn't making things easy.

Still, things are much better than they were before, and I do feel good about the future. That is until I walk by the bulletin board outside the library.

Right there in front of me, in black and white, is a flyer with James' picture on it. In big, bold letters, it says **MISSING PERSON** underneath his photo, and all I can do is stand there staring at it, willing an explanation to pop into my head as to why he would be missing.

Warren didn't... Oh, god. Lifting a hand to my chest, I try and calm myself down. I can't jump to conclusions and assume he would do something like that. He couldn't have. He beat James up, but he was alive when we left.

Like a detective, I try and piece everything together in my mind. Warren took me back to his place, and he didn't leave again, so it couldn't have been him, right? I need to ask him and see what he says and go from there.

Somehow, I get my feet to move and exit the building, walking toward the cafeteria where I'm meeting Warren and Easton for lunch. The entire walk, I'm filled with worry, wondering what the hell happened to James that night. Yes, what he did was wrong, but that doesn't mean he should die, and we all know that when someone goes missing, they generally don't just reappear alive and well.

Entering the cafeteria, the sounds of silverware clanking and people chattering meet my ears. Right away, I notice there are more of the flyers taped to the walls in here. I spot Warren sitting in our usual spot, a tray that's partially empty in front of him. Easton is sitting to his right, and Parker, his other best friend, sits across from him. There is one spot to his left open that I know is for me.

As I cross the room and see all the flyers, I suddenly start to feel like I'm in a horror film, his image appearing in front of my eyes over and over again.

"Hey, babe," Warren greets, his smile falling when he sees my horror-stricken face. I slink down into the seat beside him and start to chew on my bottom lip nervously. "What's going on? Why do you look like you're going to be sick?" he asks.

"Did you do it?" I twist in my seat and look up at Warren. His jaw is sharp, his eyes hauntingly beautiful, and I still can't believe that we're doing this.

Confusion overtakes his god-like features. "What are you talking about?"

I point to the nearest flyer and watch as he pieces the

puzzle together. The air in my lungs stills as I wait for his answer.

"I don't know what that's about. Parker took care of him." Warren looks away and pierces Parker with a hard gaze.

Parker took care of him... What does that mean?

"If this is about James going missing, I don't know what the hell happened. I waited until he woke up, and then I told him to go home. He was disoriented and could barely walk but he got up, and started walking away."

"Are you sure?" I whisper as if the FBI or someone is listening.

Parker leans across the table, "Yes, I'm sure." He whispers back in a mocking tone.

"Well, forgive me if I jump to conclusions," I roll my eyes and relax a little knowing that Warren had nothing to do with his disappearance.

"I'm an asshole, sweetheart, but not a killer." Warren leans into my ear and whispers. Goosebumps erupt across my skin and a shiver ripples down my spine. "Plus, I was with you all night, tending to your hands and knees." I know that, but the fact that we were the last people to see him doesn't sit well with me, and I know how violent Warren can get, and I was totally out of it that night.

"What happened to him then?" I ask anyone who is listening.

"Maybe he got eaten by wolves," Easton adds, and for a second, I forgot he was even sitting with us.

"Doubtful," Warren replies, rubbing at his chin.

"I can have someone check the video surveillance and see what happened after he walked off? But I'm pretty sure the police already took a look at it, so if they didn't find anything, I doubt we will," Parker suggests.

"Yeah, let's do that. I would still feel better if I knew," I agree, the knot of worry unraveling a little more in my belly.

"What you mean is, you would rather make sure I'm not lying to you?" Warren snaps.

"I didn't mean it like that," I murmur, even though it's partially true. If I'm honest, I do worry that he is lying to me.

"Why do you even care, Harper? I heard what he did to you. Warren told us. If anyone should want him to disappear, it should be you." Easton pipes up.

He's not wrong, but just because someone does something bad doesn't mean that they automatically should die or go missing. If that were the case, the world would be a much better place.

"I'm just worried. I thought maybe you guys did something, but now that I know you didn't, I wonder if something else happened to him. I know what he did was fucked up, but that doesn't mean we have to be as ruthless as he was."

"If there is anything to be found, the police will find it. No point in worrying over nothing." Parker shrugs like it's no big deal.

"You should eat something," Warren says, and I nod in agreement. I should, but I'm not sure I could stomach any food right now. I've been feeling nauseous all day long, and now the worrying is making it even worse.

"I'll grab something," I say just to appease him. Leaving my backpack on the chair, I get up and walk over to the line. Grabbing a tray, I place a slice of pizza, an apple, and a bottle of water down on it and move to the front of the line to pay.

When I return to my seat, it's just Parker and Warren sitting there. I place the tray on the table and pick the pizza slice up to take a bite, but my stomach clenches so badly it feels like all of its contents are going to come flying out of it.

Dropping the slice back down on the tray, I stare at the apple. Should I even try?

"Are you okay?" Warren asks, concern etched into his features.

"Yeah, just a stomach bug, I think. Maybe I'll go home and try and sleep it off."

"That sounds good. I'll come with you and keep you company." He wiggles his eyebrows, but I shake my head because there will be none of that. I feel like I'm going to barf all over the place.

"I'm sure that's what you'll do," Parker snorts, "keep her vagina company, more like."

Warren shrugs, "So, she's mine, and so is her pussy. I'll do with it as I please."

"Can we please go," I interrupt them before they can get into a full-on conversation about vaginas, something neither of them has.

"Yes," Warren sighs, and we get up and dump our trays. Parker says goodbye and runs off, probably to meet up with Willow.

By the time we reach the car, I'm so exhausted, I sag into my seat and let my eyes drift closed. Sleep comes to me far easier than expected, and I pray that when I wake up, this illness will be over with.

∽

I WAKE COMPLETELY DISORIENTED, my eyes scanning the nearly dark room, while the familiar scent of Warren fills my nostrils. The soft mattress cradles my body, and I lie there for a long second. The last thing I remember is falling asleep in the car. I must've really been out of it if I didn't wake up when he carried me in?

Before I can draw up a conclusion, I'm rushing from the bed, my feet sliding across the floor as I barely make it to the toilet in time to vomit. My eyes water and my throat burns as my fingers curl around the toilet bowl, while my stomach empties itself.

After a few minutes, I stop vomiting and manage to push away from the toilet. My eyes move over the contents that line the back of it, and dread consumes me when I notice the not even open box of tampons.

They sit there, taunting me while I try and do the math inside of my head. I can't be, there isn't any way. I'm on birth control...

"Oh, god..." I whisper in horror. Whirling around, I run from the bathroom and back into the bedroom. Warren isn't anywhere to be seen, and that only leaves me feeling more panicked. Walking out into the living room, I find him sitting on the couch. My heart clenches in my chest when I see his half-shadowed face.

He looks broken, shattered, and I know instantly that something is wrong.

As I pad across the floor toward him, his eyes shoot up and land on mine.

"And the queen finally wakes up." He smiles, but it's not full of joy or sunshine. It's cruel and angry. I swallow thickly and stop in my tracks, wondering if I should really tell him right now. He looks like he might kill someone, me included.

"Is everything okay?" I croak.

"Of course, come here. I've missed you. Are you feeling better?" His eyes soften, and the tension in the room eases.

"Well, actually no," I whisper. When I reach him, he

circles my waist with his hands and buries his face in my chest. He inhales deeply like I'm oxygen, and he needs me to breathe.

My heart thuds so loudly in my chest that I wonder if he can tell how scared I am right now. The pungent smell of whiskey tickles my nostrils and my stomach rolls. Oh, god, not again.

Warren pulls away and looks up at me. His eyes are glassy, and I'm guessing from the amount of whiskey missing from the bottle, he drank beyond what he needed to.

"You look like you're going to be sick again," his voice is soft and wraps around me like a wool blanket. I just need to tell him, come out with it.

He'll still love me and want me. We've been through too much for him not to, and plus, it's just a possibility. It might not even be true yet. My eyes dart from Warren and then to the wall behind him as I contemplate what I should do next.

I have to tell him...

"Warren... I think I might be... pregnant." The words fall from my lips slowly, and I watch with fear as my entire world falls apart.

"What did you just say?" He pulls away from me like I'm fire, his voice deep, his eyes dark. In a second flat, he's become the cruel bastard he was before.

"It wasn't on purpose. I didn't mean for this to happen." And I didn't, though the way Warren is looking at me right now makes me think he does.

"Pregnant?" he scoffs, his features turning even darker if that's possible. I start to shiver, the darkness in the room blocking out any light. All I can feel is his rage, his anger, it suffocates me, circles my throat like an imaginary hand and squeezes. Shoving off the couch, he towers over me, and I take a terrified step back. The man before me isn't the one I've come to know.

"It's funny, my father told me you would do this. Told me you would get pregnant and find a way to make certain I could never get rid of you." He lets out a bitter huff, and I feel the tears pooling in my eyes.

"I would never do that, Warren, and if you believe that, then you don't really know me."

He nods his head, a sinister smile pulling at his lips, "I guess I never really did know you. I thought so much of you once before, and you showed your true colors then. Now here we are again, your hand wrapped around my heart, squeezing the life out of me all over again," he reaches for the whiskey bottle, his fingers flex around the neck before he brings it to his lips.

The last thing he needs to be doing right now is drinking more.

"Warren, don't be stupid. I didn't do this to us. I wouldn't have."

His eyes turn to slits, and instantly I know I've made a mistake. In a flash, he's throwing the bottle. It crashes somewhere behind me, but that's the least of my worries. Before I can even turn to run, he has me in his grasp, his hand wrapped around my throat. He lifts me off my feet and pulls me into his chest.

Like a bug caught in a spider's web, I struggle to break free, but there is no point.

"You wouldn't have, huh?" he taunts, his face masked with burning rage. He squeezes my throat, not hard enough to hurt me but enough to grab my attention. Like a cat, I claw at his hands and chest, but my nails are nothing to him; my fight only bringing him more joy. With a snarl, he sends the next words like a knife into my heart. "Why don't you get an abortion and get the fuck out of my life."

A door opens somewhere in the house, but I can't comprehend what is going on. All I can see and feel are his words. I go slack in his arms, and he releases me, watching as I slide down his body and onto the floor. Tears stain my cheeks, and I shiver, a coldness sweeping over me. I can feel his eyes on me, feel them burning into my skin.

"When I get back you better be fucking gone, because if you aren't, I'll make you regret ever being born."

Something in my chest tightens, the pressure mounting, and I know without a doubt, it's my heart breaking, crumbling into a thousand pieces.

"What the fuck is going on?" A voice pierces the fog around my head, and I look up from where I sit on the floor, a pile of nothingness.

"Don't worry about her.... She'll be gone by the time we get back."

"Get back? What the hell happened?"

"Nothing," Warren roars, and I flinch at the sound. "We're leaving, and if you won't take me, I'll drive myself."

"Where are you going, and what about her?" I realize then that it's Cameron who is talking. My vision is blurry with tears, and though I try and shove up off the floor, I'm weak. So damn weak and broken.

"Strip club. I'm going to fuck her memory right out of me. Fuck every chick in sight and remind myself why she never mattered. Remind myself why I never should've given a fuck about her." He spits the words at me, and I feel each one clinging to my skin as if he really had spit on me.

"Warren," Cameron warns, and I can hear the sadness in his voice.

"Shut up. Take me, or I'll drive myself," Warren orders. The last thing I hear is his footsteps as he walks away from me. I thought he loved me. I thought he'd understand. I sob on to the wood floor, hating myself, and him, but hating him more because of his words.

Go get an abortion. The way he said them, the way they felt. No amount of showering or soap will ever make the stain he's left on me disappear. Even if I don't want to love Warren, or care for him ever again, I'll never be able to forget. He's taken my heart, shattered it into a million pieces, and shoved it back into my chest. I'm not sure anyone could forget someone doing that to them.

19

WARREN

Half stumbling over my own two feet, I make it inside *Night Shift*. My head is already swimming with alcohol, but I feel like I need more... much more. I don't want to think about what Harper said to me, and I definitely don't want to think about what I said to her.

"You sure you don't want to go back home?" Cameron asks.

"No, I want to be here," I tell him as we walk up to the bar. "And I want to get shit-faced. So, either join me or get the fuck away from me."

"You know I love this place, and I kinda like you... I don't know why either since you're a fucking asshole." He pauses. "But I better stay and make sure you don't get into too much trouble. Easton and I don't want to deal with your parents if you go missing."

Psh, I'm sure that's why he stays.

"Hi, there," some chick behind the bar greets me. Leaning over, she puts her elbow on the bartop, giving me a prime view of her tits. "What can I get for you?"

"I'd like to suck on your tits," I confess, making her giggle as if she is shy. I know otherwise because she keeps pushing her chest up to give me an even better view. Bitch loves the attention.

"How about we start with a drink first, and then we'll see if we can get you some tits to suck on?" She licks her lips seductively, and I nod.

"I guess we can do that... give me a long island. More long island, less ice tea."

"Coming right up. What can I get for you?" She turns her attention to Cameron.

"Beer," he gives her a short answer, making the chick frown as if she is disappointed. "You're making a mistake if you ask me."

"Good thing I'm not asking you."

Two minutes later, I have my drink in my hand, and the waitress in front of me giving me fuck me eyes. I chug the drink until the glass is more than half empty. The alcohol seemingly going straight into my bloodstream. My mind immediately going hazy.

Something soft touches my arm, and I have to force the memory of Harper's gentle touch out of my brain. When I turn to see whose hand is on my arm, I find a petite blonde. *Not Harper.* Her fingers meet my skin, sending lightning bolts of both dread and excitement through my body. I hold on to the latter, and shove the first one down, burying it deep inside my chest.

"How much for a private dance?" I let my gaze trail down her barely dressed body. She's wearing some lingerie that leaves very little to the imagination. In fact, one of her nipples is actually peeking out on one side. *Classy.* Then again, who am I to complain? I came here to get wasted and fuck some bitches.

"How long would you like your dance to be?" she asks, trailing her hand up my arm and over my shoulder. Her fingers feel like acid on my skin, but I don't care... anything to get rid of *her* memory, of her stupid voice in my fucking head.

"Maybe three or four songs long? Depending on how tight your pussy is."

The chick's eyes light up, and not surprised in the least by my proposition. These girls will do anything for money. "For you, three hundred."

"Perfect! Let's go then," I tell her, gesturing with my hands, "lead the way."

She grabs my hand and starts pulling me away. I almost trip over my feet as I glance back at Cameron one more time. He gives me a disapproving look but is smart enough not to say anything. He doesn't know what it's like to be in love and have everything fall apart. He doesn't know what it's like to have the woman of your dreams become exactly what your father said she would be. Jokes on her though. I'm going to follow through with my threat this time. I'm going to destroy her, ruin her until she's nothing, just a speck of dust.

Like a puppy, I follow the blonde to the back hall. She doesn't walk very fast on her five-inch clear high heels, so I take the time to stare at her ass while I trail behind her. It's not as full and nice as Harper's ass, but it will do. *Ugh*, I really need to get her out of my head. Maybe fucking this chick will help, then again, if it doesn't, there are plenty more women in this place.

Leading me into a small room, she switches on a dim light before closing the door.

"Sit down, sweetie." She motions toward the only chair in the room.

"Don't call me, sweetie," I growl at her as I take a seat.

"Okay, what would you like me to call you?" she asks while reaching back and undoing her bra. Her tits spring free, bouncing a little as she takes a step toward me. They're nice, but again, they aren't Harper's. The thought infuriates me, and I squeeze the arms on the chair to stop myself from lashing out.

"Don't call me anything..."

"Okay." She closes the distance between us and drops down to her knees between my legs. Her fingers flick the button on my jeans, and she is about to take my still flaccid dick out when the door suddenly flies open.

What the fuck?

The girl jumps back, and we both look up at who has come to interrupt us. I swear to god if it's Cameron... For a split second, all I see is Harper standing in the doorway, but quickly realize it's Valerie. Sweet, good, Harper would never step foot in a place like this.

"Candy, out!" she yells at the chick on her knees.

"What the hell, Val?" Candy squeals.

"Yeah, what the hell, Val?" I repeat. "Go find someone else's dick to suck."

"Warren, I wouldn't suck your dick if you offered me 10k." *Yeah, right. I bet she'd do it for half of that.* "Seriously, Candy. Get out. That's my cousin's boyfriend."

Candy shrugs, "So, everyone in here is someone's boyfriend. Never stopped you before. Plus, he's a paying customer... *my* paying customer."

Valerie's gaze turns murderous, "Out!"

Candy jumps again, a trickle of fear in her eyes. Valerie takes a step toward her, fists clenched like she's ready to throw down. Shit. I want to see this.

"Fine," Candy throws her hands up in the air. "But you owe

me, Val. This is fucked up, and you know it." She gets up from the floor, taking her bra with her, and leaves the little room. The door slams shut behind her, and Valerie crosses her arms in front of her chest, looking like she is about to give me a lecture.

God, please, save me. Harper just told me she might be... I swallow the thought down. Fuck, no. I'm not thinking about that right now.

"I'll give you five hundred bucks if you don't say whatever you are about to say and let Candy back in here," I offer, and I can see Valerie thinking about it. She wants the money, but for once in her life, her conscience wins. Fuck, of course, that has to be now. I'm about to double my offer to see how far this will go when she cuts me off before I even start talking.

"I don't want your rich boy money. I want to know what the hell is wrong with you? What did Harper ever do to you for you to treat her like this? I'm not the best person to her myself, but fuck, you really top it all. She doesn't deserve this. She doesn't deserve how you treat her."

"*How I treat her?* What about how she treats me?" My anger is growing, becoming harder and harder to ignore. If Valerie wants a fight, then we'll have one. She doesn't know all there is to know about Harper.

Valerie rolls her eyes at me. "When did Harper goody shoes ever treat anyone wrong, especially *you*. She basically worshiped the ground you walked on and even after you pulled that stunt three years ago, she somehow forgave you. Now you fuck up again?"

Unable to sit here and listen to her talk down to me any longer, I shove to my feet. A wave of nausea hits me in the gut, but I ignore it.

"Don't pretend you don't know what she did! You must

have known," I accuse her. "Your families are close, there is no way she kept that secret from you."

Valerie looks at me like I've grown a second head, "What the hell are you talking about?"

"The fucking abortion! I know she got it. She told me she wanted to wait to have sex, and then she fucked someone else and got herself pregnant." Even saying the words out loud hurt. It's like the pain will never ease, and I suppose it won't not now that she's in the same position all over again.

Valerie's eye go so wide they are basically round now. She shakes her head and covers her gaping mouth with her hand.

"Don't act so surprised. As if you didn't know."

"Oh god, Warren. You think Harper got an abortion? That's why you sent them away? Why you treated her so badly? Shit, shit, shit! This is all my fault." Valerie starts crying, and that's when I really can't handle this anymore.

"Fuck this," I say, pushing past her. I need some air, I can't fucking breathe in here. Everything is happening so fast, and it feels like I'm reliving that day all over again. Moving to stand in front of me, Valerie blocks my exit.

"Warren, I got the abortion, *me*." Valerie points at her chest. I stare down at her, trying to comprehend what she just said. "I used Harper's insurance because I didn't have any, and we looked so much alike on our ID's, so..." Valerie continues rambling on, but all the other words fade to the background when the truth is revealed.

"You... you got the abortion... not Harper?"

She nods, "Me. I got the abortion. God, Warren, Harper was still a virgin when she came here. She never cheated, never got pregnant, she never did anything wrong." I can feel the guilt in her words and see it on her face, but it's nothing compared to the agony, the pure hate I have for myself. My own personal guilt that engulfs my body.

Even with all the alcohol coursing through my veins, I feel as sober as a motherfucker, Valerie's confession shining a light on one of the darkest days of my life.

"Fuck. I fucked up." I tug at my hair in frustration. "Harper told me she might be pregnant, and I told her to get an abortion. I was so fucking angry and upset over our past, and my father pressuring me and talking shit about her." Stupid. I'm so fucking stupid. If I could kick myself in the head right now, I would. Someone should kick my ass for me.

"Warren," Valerie scolds, "you're a fucking asshole. Leave, go find her, apologize, grovel, do whatever you have to do, but make it right."

It hits me then. A knife slices through my heart, cutting the tender muscle, each thump hurts a little more than the next as I realize I may have lost her forever. "I don't know if I can fix this, Val. I don't know if there is any coming back from the things that I've done."

Valerie's hand comes out of nowhere and lands heavily on my cheek. My face turns to the side, the sting of her palm is like ice water pouring down on me. "Snap out of it. Go and find her and fix this. She loves you and I know you love her. Make things right, because after what you just told me, I won't be able to face her again unless you do."

I nod, knowing what I have to do.

It was all a lie.

The abortion.

The cheating.

I've broken her heart twice now and done some horrible things to her. I want to fall to my knees and pray that she listens to me when I tell her it was all a misunderstanding, but if I were her, I wouldn't ever forgive me. I don't deserve her, after everything I've said and done, I deserve her hate, and yet, my heart beats only for her.

Maybe she can forgive me, but forgetting all the things I've done and said to her...

No, no one could do that.

HARPER

My one suitcase sits fully packed in front of me as I wait at the bus terminal to go back to my parents' house.

I wish I had another place to go, somewhere else to run to, but there is nowhere. I need to go home and explain to them how I managed to throw my entire life away. Every chance of a successful career, gone. How am I going to go to college now? No money, no home, and now a child to take care of? I can't even take care of myself. This is... a nightmare, a true, living one.

How could I have been so stupid? How could I have trusted him again? How could I get pregnant by a monster?

Why don't you get an abortion?

His words hurt more than anything else. What would compel him to say something like that? Warren can be a horrible person, vicious and mean, but never did I think he would say something so dark and cruel.

Especially not about something that is half his, and part of both of us. What would make him ever think I would get an abortion and kill a life that belongs to us.

The sound of the bus approaching fills the streets, and I turn my head to see it heading toward me. Getting on my feet, I pull out the handle on my suitcase, so I can pull it behind me. I take about two steps toward the curb when I hear someone calling my name.

What the—

"Harper!"

I twist around to find Warren running down the sidewalk, his arms raised, his hands waving back and forth as he tries to get my attention. Bitter anger pulses through my veins. Shaking my head, I turn back and start walking to the approaching bus. It's too late. I can't and won't talk to him. Maybe someday, but not today.

"Harper," he yells again just as the bus stops, its doors opening. I'm about to step on, but my foot has barely left the ground when someone pulls me back. I try to shrug him off, but his hands are firm on my shoulders. I can feel myself melting into his touch. I want to give in, to let myself fall for anything and everything he says, but he doesn't care about me. He doesn't want me. It was all a mistake.

"Please, just let me explain. I'm so sorry, I fucked up. I thought you cheated on me and got pregnant by someone else." He pants.

Turning to face him, I can't hide my anger and sadness from him. His eyes are bloodshot, and though he smells like a liquor cabinet that's been spilled over, he seems sober. "Are you fucking serious right now? When the hell was I supposed to be with someone else? We've been together day and night for the last few weeks."

Warren shakes his head, his chest is rising and falling so

fast I worry he might be having a heart attack, "Not now, then... three years ago. I saw the doctor's bill with your name on it. It said abortion, and I thought..." I try to digest what he's saying, but I'm too angry, too sad, my give a shit is busted. Nothing can change what we've become.

"You thought I cheated on you and got an abortion? What is wrong with you? Do you know me at all? Why didn't you come talk to me? Why did you believe it in the first place? You should know that I would never do anything like that! I loved you, and you treated me like I was nothing to you time and time again." The words pour out of me. I struggle to take a breath in between.

"I'm sorry..." The words fall from his lips with ease, and I can see the guilt and shame in his features, and still, I don't care.

"I'm sorry is not good enough. This is not something I can just forgive. I can't forget the words you said to me earlier, and I don't know if I ever will. I would never get an abortion, but don't worry, you don't have to be a part of our lives. I don't want your money, and I certainly don't want you."

He staggers back like I just hit him in the face. "You don't want me?" He blinks as if he's unsure of what I just said.

Swallowing down the pain in my chest, and the thousand and one other emotions, I nod. "Right now, no, and maybe not ever. You had your chance, and you destroyed me, us. You took something beautiful and ruined it."

"I'm sorry, Harper. I'm so sorry. There is nothing I can say, nothing I can do. I can't take back the things I did. I can't rewind time. If I could, I would do it in a heartbeat. I would right all my wrongs. I would erase all the pain I caused you, everything I did to us."

*Well, you can't...*I almost say, tears stinging my eyes. It's time to end this for good. Time for me to let go. I've held onto him, and this thought that he would be mine forever for far too long. It was nothing more than a fairytale wish. Warren isn't a prince. I'm not a princess. And this isn't a fairytale. It's a nightmare, and I need to wake up. I'm going to save myself from it.

"My bus is leaving, I need to go," I tell him, grabbing onto the handle of my suitcase a little tighter.

"At least let me drive you," he offers, holding out his hand to me, but I can smell the booze from here.

"You smell like a distillery, and you shouldn't be driving anywhere, let alone with me."

He drops his hand and lowers his head in defeat. "Okay."

"Okay," I echo his words. My heart feels as if it's being ripped from my chest. I take a step away from him.

"I want to be in your life and the baby's life. Don't... don't end this forever. Don't let this be goodbye," he pleads, but in my already fragile state, there is no determining our future.

"I don't know... I really don't know if I can."

"Ma'am, I'm about to leave without you," the bus driver calls from inside the bus.

"Goodbye, Warren," I whisper as I once again find myself walking away from the man I love. The only difference, this time, I'm the one choosing to leave.

∼

A FEW DAYS have passed since I left Warren standing at the bus stop. Being home with my parents is nice, but every day is a struggle. They took the news much better than I thought they would. They are not happy about it by any means, but they don't hate me, which I was most afraid of. Mainly they are just worried about me.

All I want to do is sleep, cry, or both. My mother does what she can to console me, but I know it's futile. The only person I need and want is the one person I refuse to see right now. I just can't get over what he said to me, the words hurt me too deeply. Not to mention that for the last three years, he thought I cheated on him.

Why didn't he just talk to me? All he had to do was ask, and I would've told him the truth.

I absentmindedly cradle my stomach, like I've been doing ever since I found out. I haven't been to the doctor yet, but I did take three pregnancy tests, and every one came back positive. Curling up a little more on the couch, I think about what it will feel like when my belly grows, what it will feel like when the baby kicks for the first time...

"Hey, sweetie," my mom's voice drags me out of my daydream. My head snaps up just in time to catch her walking into the living room. I sit up, pulling the blanket a little tighter around me. I can't seem to stay warm these days.

"What's up, Mom?" I ask when I see a stack of papers in her hand.

"I just printed out some information you might want to look at," she shrugs, before taking a seat next to me.

"What is it?" I take the papers and start to look over them, quickly realizing that these are applications for grants for colleges.

"This one is for a grant specifically for single moms." She points at the top paper. "The next one is an application for financial aid at the local community college. I know it's not Blackthorn, but you can still go to school, honey. Your dad and I will help you in any way we can. Being a parent doesn't mean your world has to stop."

My heart clenches in my chest. Damn you, Mother.

Looking up from the papers, I say, "I know it doesn't stop, but I should be working and saving for when the baby is born. College is still an option, but not until the baby is older."

"Harper," my mother starts, and I already know what she's going to say, so I politely cut her off.

"Mom, I'm not going to take any money from you and Dad. I'll figure out a way to make things work, but it won't be by taking from you."

Even though I know she wants to say something, she doesn't. She just presses her lips into a firm line and puts the papers on the side table next to the couch.

The awkward silence that follows is interrupted by the doorbell ringing.

"I'll get it," my dad calls before my mom even makes a move. A few seconds later, he pops back into the room, but he's not alone. Valerie is hot on his heels, a desperate look in her eyes. Dear god, what happened? I feel the question burning at the tip of my tongue. Valerie never comes to visit my parents, which means she knew I would be here, which means...

"Hi," she squeaks, and my mother jumps up to greet her, a wide smile on her face. Wrapping her arms around her, she pulls my cousin into a tight hug. "Hey, Aunt Marie. Sorry, I haven't come to visit in so long," Valerie admits shamefully.

"It's okay, I know you're busy with work and stuff. Come in, sit down. Do you want some coffee? Something to eat?" My mom bombards her with questions while my dad disappears into the other room quietly.

"Just some coffee would be great," Valerie smiles. My mom nods and scurries away and into the kitchen. As soon as both of my parents are out of earshot, I pin her with a glare and bombard her with my own questions.

"What's wrong? Why are you here? Did something happen?"

"Harper, I feel like this is all my fault. If it weren't for me using your insurance, this whole mess never would've happened."

I frown, "Val... it's not your fault. He should've talked to me."

Valerie nods as if she understands, "I know, but still if it weren't for my stupid decisions, you and Warren would still be together." She sounds sad, beyond sad. Kinda, like me.

"I don't know if Warren and I can fix what we had."

"You two belong together." Her eyes dart to the floor, "The truth is, I've always been kind of jealous of you. What you and Warren have is special. Don't throw this away. He wants to take care of you and the baby."

I want to be mad, but I'm weak. Weak for Warren, weak for the possibility of a future together. All I've ever wanted was him, but can I forgive him for what he said, what he did?

"Can you at least talk to him? Just give him a chance to apologize?" Valerie sounds desperate, and if she's desperate, that means this is bad.

"I think you should," my mom pops her head in from the kitchen. "I always liked Warren when you guys were together, he was sweet to you, and he made you happy."

Oh, if only she knew how things have changed.

"I don't know..." It feels like I'm being tugged in two directions. One that's telling me not to give in, and one that's saying you're already his. My eyes fall to my flat belly. We're having a baby together, another human, that will need both of us.

It's his baby too, and you might as well make things easier for yourself.

My mom nods her head as if she actually knows what I'm

thinking about. I know it would be easier on my parents if I let Warren help out.

"All you have to do is listen to him talk. You don't even have to respond if you don't want to. Just hear him out..." It all weighs heavily on my shoulders like cement blocks. "Do it for the baby," Valerie adds a second later.

"Fine," I whisper in defeat, praying like hell that this isn't going to be a mistake that blows up in my face. I've already made too many mistakes when it comes to Warren. I can't keep doing this to myself, and now my baby.

"Awesome," Valerie cheers and pushes to her feet. "Let's go then."

"*Go?* Like... when? As in now?"

"Yes, let's go!" Valerie pulls me to my feet. The blanket falls away, and the cool air that kisses my skin makes me shiver.

"Okay, hold on. I need my shoes and a jacket." I guess now is as good of a time as ever, no point in delaying the inevitable.

My dad appears out of nowhere, holding my jacket out to me, while my mom brings me my shoes. *Are they trying to get rid of me?* I slip into my shoes and pull on my jacket, zipping it all the way to the top.

"Did you drive here?"

"Yes, I borrowed someone's car, come on," Val urges, pulling me toward the door. In a rush, I tell my parents good-bye. They both tell me that they love me, and I open my mouth to reply, but she basically drags me through the door before I can say anything.

"We've got time, Val," I gasp.

As soon as I'm out the door, I realize why she hurried me outside. Right there, only a few feet away, Warren stands. Leaning against the inside of the fence, he straightens when he sees me. It's hard to breathe, to look at him, but at the same time, it feels like the planets have aligned.

"Harper..." The way my name rolls off his tongue, it makes my knees shake.

I spent the last few days hating him, trying to forget him. Forget his stupidly handsome face, his smile, and the way he wraps his arms around me. I tried to forget the way he smells when I bury my face into his chest and the way his lips taste when they are pressed against my own. Every single one of those memories come rushing back all at once.

I know I shouldn't forgive him so easily, maybe I shouldn't forgive him at all. But right now, all I want to do is run into his arms and hold onto him until my limbs hurt. He's the only one that can make the pain go away but is the very reason the ache exists.

"I don't expect you to forgive me, listen to me, or even want me after this, but I have to tell you how sorry I am. I know I fucked up. I don't want your pity, and you're not to blame." He blows out a breath, "But I can't live without you. You're everything to me. I know I've done a shit job showing it, but I thought..."

My brain tells me not to listen to a word he says and walk back inside. But everything else in me; my gut, my heart, every fiber of my being, tells me to forgive him. I can't stop myself from walking toward him, or from wrapping my arms around him and burying my face in his firm chest. Inhaling, I let his unique scent fill my lungs. A calmness washes over me then.

His arms come around me, caging me in, pulling me deeper, not in a physical sense but emotionally. I'm drowning in Warren and have been since I was a kid. It's only ever been him, and though he's done wrong, hurt me, and said horrible things, they were under a false pretense. He thought wrongly of me, and because of his pain, he lashed out. He wanted revenge, and I can't fault him for that. I can't fault him for protecting himself. As angry, and sad, and hurt as I am, I can't let those emotions define me, define what I have with this man. Sighing into his chest, I know it will take me time to forgive him, but I will.

His touch promises without words to never let me go again. For the first time in days, I feel warm. The coldness that lived in my bones is gone, and only now do I realize that it was the emptiness and loneliness that kept me cold. He is my home, my warmth, my happiness.

"I missed you," I mumble into his sweater.

"You have no idea how much I missed you. I was so scared that you wouldn't forgive me. Please come home with me, back to Blackthorn. I'll do whatever you want. Tell me what you need, and it's yours. I'm yours. All of me. I've always been yours, Harper. Please, give me another chance, and I won't let you regret it. I love you..."

"I love you too, Warren. And I'll forgive you." I barely get to finish my sentence before Warren's hands find my waist, and he lifts me off the ground. With my feet dangling in the air, he holds me so tightly to his body, I can't move. When I let out a grunt, he releases me, a horrified look on his face.

"Oh, god, shit. Did I squish you? Did I squish the baby?" I want to laugh but hold back. Warren, as a father, is going to be something else.

"I'm fine," I smile. "And the baby is like the size of a bean, I don't think there is any squishing to do yet."

With a hopeful tone, he asks, "So you'll come back with me?"

"Yes, I'll come back with you," I answer, not caring to make him sweat it out. Going forward, I don't want to hold any anger toward him.

He wraps his arms around me again, but this time much gentler. Kissing the top of my head, he says, "Good, 'cause I don't think I could live without you. You're a part of me, Harper, and you always have been. When I lost you the first time, I thought I might die, and after I realized I had fucked up this second time, I didn't expect another chance. But I swear to you and our unborn baby, that I'll do the right thing. I'll cherish and care for you both. Forever. For always."

EPILOGUE

Warren

The keys to our brand new three-bedroom house sit like a damn brick in my jeans pocket. Harper hasn't the first clue what is going on. She thinks we're going for ice cream at the sugar shack. Hopefully, she doesn't go into labor because of this surprise. It took a shit-ton of work and a lot of time to get everything together, but I know without a doubt that it will be worth it.

"You look lost in thought, are you okay?" Harper questions from the passenger seat, a smile that warms every inch of my body on her pretty pink lips.

"Of course, I'm okay. I have you and our little girl. There's nothing else in the world I could want."

That makes Harper smile even more, and I can't imagine what her face is going to look like when she sees the house.

I drive right past the sugar shack and down the ways a little more before turning right and into the subdivision.

"Where are we going? This doesn't look like an ice cream place?" Harper pouts, and I chuckle as I drive a little further. Our perfect two-story house comes into view, and I continue driving until I reach the driveway. I pull in and park the car. I don't say anything else to Harper but can feel her staring boulders into my face. Inside, I'm bubbling over with excitement. It's been a long seven months together, and I've busted my ass to ensure that she can trust me.

As I get out of the car and walk around to the passenger side to help her out, she wrinkles her nose at me.

"Warren, you better start talking. Whose house is this?" Again, I say nothing and grab her hand and start walking up the driveway and toward the huge front wooden door.

Our first home.

Once we reach the doorstep, Harper tugs her hand out of mine and crosses her arms over her chest. "If you don't start talking, I'm going to get mad."

"You're cute when you're mad."

"Warren," she whines, using her angry voice, which only makes me want to irritate her more, so I can hear her whine again.

"Whose house do you think this is?"

"I don't know." She turns to stare at the front door, and I slip my hand into my pocket and pull out the keys. "What are you doing?" she questions. I bring the key to the front lock and open the door.

"Welcome home, baby," I lean down and whisper into her ear.

A gasp escapes her lips before she grabs onto my hand and turns to face me, "You're lying, this isn't ours."

The look on her face makes me smile. I cannot believe that I was able to keep this a secret, which makes that look one-hundred percent worth it.

"I'm not. It's ours. This is where we will live, you, me, and our daughter and any future children we decide to have."

Surprise paints her features, "Oh, my god, Warren. How did you do this? Can we afford this?" Of course, with her emotions heightened her beautiful eyes mist over.

"Yes, we can afford it, and don't worry about how I did it. Just know that I did it for you and the baby. We're going to be so happy and safe here."

She nods, her throat bobbing, most likely clogged with emotion. Taking her hand in mine, I guide her into the house. I close the door behind us and listen with joy as her eyes scan over every inch of the place. The entire house is furnished with brand new furniture, appliances, and everything that we could need to start living here today.

"You did all of this?"

"Yes, now let me show you around the house. I want you to see everything."

Especially the nursery. We do a full walkthrough of the house, and I save the baby room, and our bedroom for last, knowing it'll be the two things that will push her over the edge. Stopping at the nursery, I press a kiss to her forehead and open the door.

Like a child that cannot be contained, she walks into the room and starts touching every little thing, mumbling under her breath about how beautiful it is, and how the colors match, and I got the baby crib she wanted.

It's such an amazing moment and one that makes me smile so big my cheeks hurt. When she's finally done touching every piece of furniture, she walks over to me, tears in her eyes.

"How did you do all of this?"

"Magic," I wink and wrap my arms around her. Our baby girl takes that moment to kick, and we both laugh. There is nothing better in this life, nothing at all. "There is one more thing I want to show you." Gently, I interlace our fingers and pull her out of the room and across the hall and into our bedroom. "And this is where said magic happens."

Harper starts laughing, a hand resting on her swollen belly. God, she's beautiful, so beautiful.

"What about all our other stuff at your place?"

"We can go through it. Keep what you want and get rid of the other stuff."

"Okay," she pulls away and walks over to the bed. She sits down on the edge, and I shove my hands into my pockets. Seeing everything come together, it's more than I ever could've imagined it to be.

"Should we test the bed out?" She wiggles her eyebrows at me, and I lick my lips. Is she kidding? Does she even know me?

"Well, yeah. Either now or later. Though, as you know… I'm always hungry for you." I'm not lying, I can never get enough of her, it doesn't matter how many times a day we fuck, I can always go one more time. Luckily, Harper seems to be just as insatiable as me, especially since I knocked her up.

"How do you want me?' she asks seductively, and I almost come in my pants right then.

"Naked and on all fours," I order and watch as she takes off her clothes slowly. I make quick work of my own clothes, fisting my cock as soon as it springs free. She is so fucking beautiful with her stomach round and swollen, I don't know what it is about her being pregnant, but somehow, she makes me even crazier than before.

She knows it too.

Harper climbs onto the bed, moving like a lioness on the prowl. My sweet, innocent, Harper is gone. Crawling across the mattress, she gets on all fours, arching her back and sticking out her ass, so I get to see her pussy on full display.

"You're a dirty girl, aren't you? You're already soaked for me."

She moans in response, wiggling her ass like a red flag, and I'm the fucking bull.

"Do you want me to fuck you?"

"Yes, please," she begs breathlessly, beckoning me to come to her.

I get on the bed and position myself behind her. All I want to do is slam my cock into her tight cunt and lose myself, but I want to do something else first. Placing my hands on each of her ass cheeks, I spread them apart, opening her up to me. Leaning down, I dive in between those folds, licking her once from her clit all the way up to her perfect little asshole.

Using my tongue, I massage her there a few moments before I press into the puckered hole. She pushes her ass back, right into my face as she mewls into the mattress. I know she likes this. Loves this actually. Ass play is her new favorite thing. My dirty girl.

I tongue fuck her asshole for a few minutes until my saliva drips down her cunt, mingling with her arousal, and I can't take it any longer. My dick is so hard it hurts, and if I don't get relief soon, my balls are going to explode.

Straightening up, I align my dick with her pussy and slam inside in one swoop. She cries out in pleasure, screaming my name into the pillow. *Fuck*, she is so tight in this position, I'm not going to last long. Judging by her moans, she won't need much longer either.

Taking my thumb, I circle her still wet asshole and slip it

inside gently. She pushes back, making me sink in deeper, all while I fuck her pussy.

When I feel her thighs quivering and her walls tightening around my cock, I know she is fucking close. I remove my thumb from her ass and replace it with two fingers. Going deep, I rub the thin wall connecting her two channels. She moans so loudly, I'm pretty sure the neighbors hear her.

"Yeah, that's it, come for me, Harper. Be my good little slut." That last bit of dirty talk drives her over the edge. She goes off like fireworks. Her pussy strangling my cock, and her ass holds onto my finger. That combination sets my own release off.

My balls tighten, and mindless pleasure shoots through my body. Every single muscle tightens before completely relaxing.

Together we sag to the mattress. Both breathing heavily, our bodies sweaty, sticky, and absolutely sated... for this moment, at least.

"I like having sex in our new bed," Harper whispers after a few moments of silence. She sounds sleepy, so I pull the blanket over her.

"You like having sex everywhere," I chuckle, tucking her in.

"That's true. I don't care where I have sex as long as it's with you."

"Good, 'cause there is not going to be anyone else for you, ever. You and me. Like it was always supposed to be."

The End

Next in this series is Hurting You
Keep reading for a sneak peak...

NEXT IN THIS SERIES

ALSO BY THE AUTHORS

CONTEMPORAY ROMANCE

The Bet
The Dare
The Secret
The Vow

Also by the Authors

Bayshore Rivals
(Reverse Harem Bully Romance)

When Rivals Fall
When Rivals Lose
When Rivals Love

***

DARK ROMANCE

The Rossi Crime Family
(Dark Mafia Romance)

Convict Me
Protect Me
Keep Me

Also by the Authors

Guard Me
Tame Me
Remember Me

The Blackthorn Elite
(Dark Bully Romance)

Hating You
Breaking You
Hurting You

***

EROTIC STANDALONES

Runaway Bride
FREE NOVELLA

There Captive
(A Dark Reverse Harem)

Beck and Hallman
BLEEDING HEART ROMANCE

- **f** CASSANDRAHALLMAN
  AUTHORJLBECK

- **◉** CASSANDRA_HALLMAN
  AUTHORJLBECK

- **BB** CASSANDRAHALLMAN
  JLBECK

Printed in Great Britain
by Amazon